# D.R. GRAHAM

D.R. Graham lives in Vancouver, Canada with her husband. She worked as a social worker with at-risk youth prior to becoming a therapist in private practice. Her novels deal with issues relevant to young adults in love, transition, or crisis.

www.drgrahambooks.com

Other books by D.R. Graham:

*Put It Out There* (Britannia Beach Series)
*And Then What?* (Britannia Beach Series)
*Rank*
*One Percenter* (Noir et Bleu MC Series)
*The Handler* (Noir et Bleu MC Series)
*It Is What It Is* (Noir et Bleu MC Series)
*The Noir et Bleu* (Noir et Bleu MC Series)
*Hit That And You're Dead*

# What Are The Chances?

Britannia Beach

## D.R. GRAHAM

A division of HarperCollins*Publishers*
www.harpercollins.co.uk

Harper*Impulse* an imprint of
HarperCollins*Publishers*
1 London Bridge Street
London SE1 9GF

www.harpercollins.co.uk

A Paperback Original 2016

First published in Great Britain in ebook format by Harper*Impulse* 2016

A catalogue record for this book
is available from the British Library

ISBN: 9780008145200

Set in Minion by Palimpsest Book Production Limited, Falkirk, Stirlingshire

Printed and bound in Great Britain

For Charlotte

# CHAPTER 1

The bells on the front door of the Inn jingled and my best friend Sophie Sakamoto walked through the archway into the dining room. The breakfast guests all glanced in her direction, probably because her black boots, black leggings, dark sunglasses, and black tank-top dress under a black-leather jacket were an unexpected style in my tiny historic village. She looked like she just rolled out of a crypt somewhere.

We hadn't seen each other in almost three weeks, which was the longest time we'd ever been apart, so I screeched and rushed over to hug her. Despite the fact it was too early in the morning for her to show enthusiasm, she let me smother her with affection. "Welcome home."

"You too," she said, strangled by my embrace. "But don't tell me anything about Europe. It will only make me depressed that I didn't go with you. Not. One. Word."

"It's not like you were sitting at home doing nothing. A cross-country tour with the band is a big deal."

She rolled her eyes and shook her head to disagree. "Not compared to the UK, France, and Italy. I don't want to know how much fun you had."

I pretended to lock my lips with a key, then topped up a cup

1

of coffee for a guest and filled one for Sophie with cream. "When you said you would drop by to say hi on your way to the gig, I didn't expect to see you this early."

"Doug forgot to tell me the show's in Victoria not Vancouver. We have to catch the ferry at noon. I'm not happy about the early wake-up call, obviously. And apparently we're staying tomorrow night, too, just to party. Sorry you and I can't hang out until I get back. Is that okay?"

"Of course. A gig in Victoria is exciting. Congratulations. Do you want something to eat?"

"No thanks, but the guys do. Is your grandpa around?"

"No. I let him sleep in since he had to do everything all by himself while I was in Europe."

"Not. One. Word." Sophie pointed at me in a mock threat. "I seriously don't want to know how awesome Paris and London and Rome were."

"Sorry." I smiled and squeezed her shoulders. "The buffet is almost gone. Tell the guys to come in through the kitchen. I'll make them something else."

Sophie raised the cup of coffee in silent thanks before she went out to the parking lot to let the band know they could come in for breakfast.

The last two tables of guests were finished eating, so I cleared their dishes and headed through the swing doors into the kitchen. My neighbour Kailyn was seated at the pastry table, helping herself to an entire can of whipped cream. Kailyn, her dad, and her brother Trevor had lived next door since I was five and they almost always ate breakfast at the Inn. Although Kailyn was twenty-one and one year older than Trevor was, she looked five years younger and acted ten years younger because of her special needs.

"You can't eat that much whipped cream," I said.

"Yes I can."

"It'll make you sick."

After some contemplation, she used her hand and slid half the fluffy white mound off the waffle and onto the metal pastry table. "Trevor came home last night."

"Yeah, I heard his motorbike," I said as I cleaned up the mess.

Trevor and I had a complicated relationship. We had been best friends as kids, but when he went to high school two years before I did, we drifted apart. Then, in my grade-eleven year, I developed a giant crush on him. It was weird. I loved him. I thought he loved me. But nothing happened between us. In the fall, I started grade twelve and he moved down to Vancouver to live on campus at the University of British Columbia. For my whole senior year he came home to Britannia Beach on weekends, but he was always busy with Search and Rescue, his friends, or spending time with Kailyn. I eventually gave up on the hope of a romantic relationship developing between us and moved on.

"Kailyn, did Trevor say he was going to come over for breakfast?"

"He left. With Murphy." She opened a teen magazine and turned the pages, then, without elaborating, changed the subject to talk about her most recent pop-star crush, "Riley Rivers has a sister. Her name is Amy."

Unlike some of Kailyn's favourite heartthrobs, I actually knew a little about Riley. He was talented, but what I thought was even more impressive was the charity work he did in third-world countries when he wasn't on tour. I was interested in finding out more about him, but before we had a chance to continue the conversation the band piled into the kitchen and spread out on stools around the pastry table. Sophie's boyfriend Doug hugged me. "Welcome home, Deri. How was your trip?"

Sophie shot me a cautionary glare.

"It sucked," I said loudly for her benefit, then winked at Doug and whispered, "It was the most amazing experience of my life."

Sophie groaned. Doug chuckled and hugged her. "Don't worry, babe. When the band makes it big we'll tour all over the world."

"From Winnipeg to New York, then Tokyo," she muttered.

"Exactly." Doug pointed at her to cement the point. "Positive intentions."

"Make it happen." She shoved his shoulder. "I'm going to be pissed until it does."

"On it," he promised before he encouraged Kailyn to stand and dance with him while he sang her a Riley Rivers song.

"Doug's in a good mood," I said to Sophie as I made scrambled eggs.

"Yeah. Weird, right? He's been perma-happy since we went on tour. And I don't know why since life on the road kind of bites." She flicked my arm and raised one eyebrow in a suggestive way. "We passed Murphy and Trevor going the other way on the highway. When did he get home from California?"

"Last night." I served the eggs onto five plates and slid them across the table one at a time.

"That's interesting timing. Did he come over for breakfast?" She braced her boot against the side of the cupboards and leaned until her stool teetered on only two feet, balancing by resting her back against the wall.

"Nope." I leaned my elbows on the table.

"Too bad," she made a purring sound in her throat. Doug gave her a pseudo-offended look, so she said, "Don't worry, babe. The ruggedly handsome outdoorsy type doesn't do it for me."

He laughed.

She kicked my leg. "I have a good feeling. I think you and Trevor are going to finally get together this summer."

"You should probably let go of that hope. It definitely wasn't meant to be. He has a girlfriend now."

"What? When did that happen?"

I shrugged, not really sure about the details. "Kailyn mentioned something about it a couple of months ago. I also overheard Murphy and his brother going on once about how hot she is."

"Hey, Doug!" Sophie shouted across the kitchen and inter-

4

rupted the guys talking. "Did you know Trevor's been seeing someone?"

His smile disappeared and his eyes shifted between Sophie and me. "I. Uh." He frowned, trying to figure out the best way to answer the question. "I." He winced. "Maybe."

She shook her head and threw a spoon that bounced off his chest. "You need to mention shit like that."

"Sorry. I didn't know about that rule." He chuckled. "Next time I'll tell you right away."

"You, of all people, know ignorance of the law is not a defence. I'll deal with you later."

He smiled in a way that made it seem like he was looking forward to whatever her wrath for withholding information was going to be. He winked at her, then rejoined the conversation with the guys.

Sophie pulled a bottle of purple nail polish out of her pocket. "I don't get why Trevor still hasn't asked you out. You were single all year."

I twirled a chunk of my hair around my finger repeatedly. "He obviously had better options. Her name is Lindy."

"Lindy Jacobsen wants to make a baby with Trevor," Kailyn said.

"See." My face unintentionally grimaced at the visual of Trevor and Lindy doing it.

Sophie laughed as she applied a coat of dark-purple over her already black nails. "Don't give up yet, Deri. You have the rest of the summer to get in his pants and make him forget he ever met her."

"I don't want to. I accepted the scholarship in Toronto. There's no point to having a summer fling that can't go anywhere after that."

"Oh, there's a point to a summer fling. Trust me."

"Not with Trevor." I shook my head. "I would want more if I ever got together with him. But." I paused for dramatic effect. "I heard Mason is back in town. I wouldn't mind a summer fling with him. He would definitely be a nice way to soak up every second of the last summer I will ever spend in Britannia Beach. Fun. Carefree."

"Mason?" Her lips puckered into a fish face and she glanced up at the ceiling as she thought back. "Cartwright? I almost forgot about that guy."

"I didn't." I lifted my eyebrows in an animated way and smiled.

She wrinkled her nose, not as enthusiastic about the option of Mason as I was.

Thunder cracked outside. When I glanced out the window a series of completely random images flicked through my mind: It was pouring rain. I fell and my body jolted from the painful impact. Rocks and water flooded towards me. Fast. Lots of rushing water. Then freezing-cold darkness engulfed me. I couldn't breathe. I was drowning.

"Derian." Sophie gently placed her hand on my wrist. She was one of the few people outside my family and Trevor's family who knew I sometimes experienced intuitive visions. She also knew that it usually predicted something traumatic. She studied my expression as she waited for me to tell her what I'd seen.

My heart pounded. My breath was still ragged, as if I had actually fallen and almost drowned.

"What happens?" Sophie whispered so the guys wouldn't hear.

"I don't know. It felt like someone drowning. It was too vague, as usual. Just rain and water and, ugh, nothing useful about who, when, or where." I glanced over at the guys in the band to see if any of them had noticed me have my brain glitch. Fortunately, they were busy washing their dishes and not paying attention. I lowered my voice and said, "I didn't have any visions the entire time I was in Europe. Maybe they only happen when I'm near something I'm emotionally connected to, like Britannia Beach."

"Or Trevor," she said.

Hmm. That hadn't occurred to me, but it was possible. Trevor and Britannia Beach went hand in hand, so it was hard to separate which one had more influence. My unusually heightened intuition was something I inherited from my grandmother's grandmother and it started when I was about three. When I was young, I'd do things that could be explained as just coincidental, like get up to go meet my dad at the door before his truck even turned in off the highway. Or I would insist on wearing rain boots on a sunny morning in preparation for the unforecasted storm that inevitably showed up in the afternoon. I thought everyone could see things before they happened and I was shocked when Trevor told me he couldn't. As I got older, I almost only ever saw traumatic things before they happened. And although my visions sometimes helped to prevent the bad thing from happening, they didn't always. And that was hard to deal with. If I moved away and stopped having the visions, it would be both a relief and a weird loss.

Kailyn interrupted my thoughts when she randomly said to Sophie, "I like your red lips and black eyeliner. You look pretty."

"Thank you, Kailyn. Could you please tell my mother that?" Sophie slid her sunglasses down from the top of her head and tipped the stool onto all four feet again.

"Are the sunglasses really necessary in the rain?" I asked.

"I have a rock-star image to uphold. Apparently we're destined to go on a world tour." She stood and pointed at me threateningly. "You better have some sort of juicy romance details by the time I get back. This is your last hoorah." The band thanked me for breakfast and filed out the kitchen door. Sophie paused at the doorframe. "Hey, Kailyn, if we see Riley Rivers we'll tell him you want to marry him. Okay?"

Ecstatic, Kailyn grinned and pressed her fists tightly against her chubby, freckled cheeks as she nodded.

"And Deri, if you don't get busy with someone soon, I will put up a billboard on the highway to advertise that you're open for business." She winked. "Okay?"

"Break a leg. Literally," I sneered.

"Psychics shouldn't say shit like that."

"Oh my God." I stood abruptly and the stool scarped across the linoleum. "Sorry. You're right. What if my vision has something to do with your trip? Maybe you guys shouldn't go."

"You saw rain and water. It's kind of vague."

"And someone falling and drowning."

"We'll drive carefully over bridges. And I'll check the location for life vests on the ferry. I promise. Try to have a vision about the band getting discovered by a music exec."

"Sophie, seriously. Maybe you shouldn't go."

"We'll be fine, and if we're not, at least you can take comfort in the fact that you tried to stop me."

Knowing there was no way to convince her to not take risks, I shook my head and sighed. "Be careful."

"I will, and if I meet a girl named Lindy, I'll kick her ass for you."

"Aw, you're so sweet. But I don't care that he has a girlfriend. I moved on, remember?"

"Yeah. Sure you did."

"Seriously. I have. Any idea when you're going to move on and let the pipe dream go, too?"

She flashed me a peace sign and disappeared out the door. I watched through the windows as she ran back through the rain to the van, covering her long, black hair with her arms. A thick, grey mist had rolled in over the mountain and gave the dark silhouettes of the giant cedars and Douglas firs a ghost-like appearance. The fog swallowed the van as it drove away, which I hoped wasn't a bad omen. I gave Kailyn a plate of food to take next door to her dad and promised to play checkers with her in the afternoon. She exited out the kitchen door and walked across the parking lot to their house with big, wide strides that made her body sway exaggeratedly from side to side. The rain didn't seem to bother her.

As I headed to the lobby, my phone buzzed with a text. It was from Trevor: *Save me a muffin?*

Considering that I had moved on, receiving a text from him really shouldn't have had the effect on my body that it did. To force my old feelings for him back below the surface I reminded myself he had a girlfriend and I was leaving for Toronto at the end of the summer. Then I responded: *They're not as good when they're not hot out of the oven.*

Trevor's reply dinged right away: *Been thinking about your famous apple cinnamon muffins the whole time you were gone. Looking forward to it.*

I smiled and shook my head as I typed back: *Weird that you spend that much time thinking about muffins.*

*Did you miss me?*

My breathing halted and I stared at the screen of my phone. Why? Why did he ask things like that? How is a person supposed to respond to a question like that? No, I didn't miss you because you have a girlfriend and I've actually been trying to forget about my feelings for you all year. Or, yes, I missed you. I miss you every single day. I always have, and I can't imagine ever not missing you.

Before I had a chance to come up with an appropriate response that couldn't be misread, my phone rang. It was him, so I answered.

"Welcome home," he said. His smile was audible.

"You too." Not wanting to touch on the "did you miss me?" question I said, "I was hoping you'd come over for breakfast so I could hear how the road trip was."

"Yeah, sorry. I want to hear about your trip, too. But we have a Search and Rescue training thing all day today. It starts in a minute." I waited for him to ask me to hang out or meet up somewhere, but instead he asked, "Are you still planning to go to U of T?"

"Uh." When I first received the acceptance letters from both schools, I had been leaning towards the University of British Columbia to stay close to everyone. But the University of Toronto offer also came with a scholarship, so the financial factors, combined with my reluctance to move in with my mom in Vancouver, pushed me to make an impulsive decision to move across the country. "I accepted the scholarship at U of T." After a weird silence I added, "But since UBC accepted me, too, I can still transfer. I have until the end of July to withdraw from U of T if I decide not to take the scholarship."

He was quiet for a few seconds before he said, "Well, you should probably take the money, but if you decide to stay in Vancouver and go to UBC, you can live at your mom's during the week and I'll drive you up here on weekends."

Right. He hadn't heard the news about the Inn yet. And saying it out loud made it real, which I had hoped to avoid for as long as possible. But he was going to find out eventually anyway, so I said, "The sale of the Inn went through last week. The new owners take over in September. Whichever school I choose I will have to move out of Britannia Beach."

"Oh."

I waited for him to say more because "oh" wasn't enough of a reaction to tell how he felt about it.

After another long silence he said, "I've gotta go, Deri. The training is starting. Is it all right if we talk later?"

Talking about it probably wasn't going to make it any easier, but I said, "Yeah. Okay."

He said goodbye. I sighed and hung up as thunder cracked outside and the rain pounded down harder. Scenes from my vision flashed through my mind again and I panicked when I realized it might have had something to do with Trevor training in the storm. My hands fumbled to call him back, but he didn't answer.

# CHAPTER 2

"Excuse me, miss. What is there to do in Britannia Beach when it's raining?" a guest asked me as his two kids climbed on the antique chairs and rolled around on the wood lobby floor.

I hesitated because the real answer for a family with two little kids was, not much, but obviously I wasn't going to say that. My thumb tapped the send button on the text I wrote to Trevor. I told him about my vision and pleaded with him to be careful. He had witnessed my visions in the past and would definitely take the warning seriously, but I was worried he wouldn't get the message in time. The man lifted his eyebrows, impatient for me to answer his question.

"The old copper mine runs tours from the village." I pointed over my shoulder in the general direction of the mine.

"We did that yesterday."

"Okay, uh." The area was known for outdoor activities like skiing, rock climbing, river rafting, mountain biking, and kite sailing. Even if it had been sunny and warm, none of those would have worked for a young family anyway. "If the rain lets up, you can go to the beach on the other side of the highway and explore the tidal pools along the shore to search for starfish and crabs. We also have hundreds of hiking trails up the mountain behind

11

us. You won't notice the rain that much when you're under the canopy of the forest. The waterfalls you'll pass and the views of Howe Sound and the Tantalus mountain range are worth the trek. I'll find a map for you." I crouched behind the front desk to get him some brochures. But then it hit me that they might be the subjects of my vision and sending them out into the wilderness might be a bad idea. "As you can see, there is a restaurant and a few souvenir shops here in Britannia Beach." I pointed to the horseshoe of old buildings that lined the perimeter of our parking lot next to Trevor's house, hoping maybe they'd be interested in a safe, quiet day close to the Inn.

The guest peered out the window at the ocean on one side of the highway. Then he turned his head to look at the base of the mountain jammed right up behind our little old mining village. His forehead started to sweat as if he was getting claustrophobic or something.

He wasn't impressed, so I grasped for ideas. "There's shopping, a bowling alley, and a movie theatre in Squamish. It's a short drive north on the highway."

His face relaxed a little and he took in the information about Squamish. "Thanks," he said, looking kind of like he wished they had chosen Mexico instead of the rugged Canadian wilderness as their summer vacation destination.

There wasn't anything I could do to prevent whatever bad thing was going to happen if I didn't know what that thing was. Or where it happened. Or when it happened. Or who it happened to. I tried not to worry about the vision, although it wasn't working that well. Once the majority of guests had either gotten in their cars or gone back to their rooms, I carried a tray of the breakfast leftovers down the hall to my granddad's room. He was still sleeping. I opened the blinds, which didn't make the room that much brighter since the sky was so thick with black clouds.

"Good morning," I said at a volume gentle enough not to startle him, but loud enough to hear without his hearing aids.

He rolled over and patted down the few wispy white hairs left on the top of his head. "Oh dear. What time is it? Is the coffee brewing?" He got out of bed and put on a robe over his pyjamas.

"Everything is taken care of," I reassured him. "Everyone has already eaten and I'm finished the clean-up too."

"Oh Derian. Why didn't you wake me earlier?" He hooked his glasses behind his ears and squinted at the clock, wondering why the alarm hadn't gone off.

"I turned your alarm off. You deserve a day to rest once in a while." I laid out some clean clothes on his bed. "Taking it easy will prepare you for retirement."

"I can't take today off. Alan and Paula are coming by this morning."

"The new owners?"

"Yes. I'm supposed to give them an orientation today. They also want to come in and do shifts while we're here so they can get the hang of how to run things."

"That's a good idea." It made me feel better to know they were eager to learn. Out of all the people who could have bought the Inn I was grateful it was a family who would retain its old charm and continue to run it the same way we always had.

"They're going to be a good fit. I can feel it," he said.

"I feel it too." I rested my hand on his shoulder and kissed his cheek as I reached over to steal a piece of toast and peanut butter off the tray. "But since we're technically still on the clock until the end of the summer, I should get back to the front desk. Enjoy your breakfast." I left his room and headed back to the lobby.

Two more families who were desperate to entertain their kids during the storm took brochures on the attractions in Squamish. Growing up in an ancient rain forest, I was brought up with the attitude that there was no such thing as bad weather, just bad clothing. But even I had to admit it was a particularly dreary day. Curling up next to the fireplace with a good book appealed to me.

As I scanned the list of check-ins for the afternoon, three trucks, all black, pulled into the parking lot—one after the other in a convoy—a Hummer, a Mercedes G Class, and a Range Rover. I knew who they were and a jolt of excitement slammed through me when the driver of the Range Rover got out and crossed the parking lot towards the front door of the Inn.

I ripped the elastic out of my ponytail and shook my head to make my hair fall straight over my shoulders and down my back. My reflection in the black computer screen reminded me that I still looked like I just rolled out of bed. At best. Oh well. Too late. The driver of the Range Rover, Mason Cartwright, stepped through the door into the lobby. He ran his hands through his wet caramel-brown hair and pushed it back off his forehead. He smiled. "Hi Derian."

"Hey." Saying something more elaborate would have been helpful to at least pretend to be articulate. Unfortunately, my lips felt as if I had gone to the dentist and then got caught in a blizzard.

"How have you been?"

I opened my mouth, but no sound came out. I tried again and was able to spit out, "Um. Good. You're home."

He chuckled at my blatant statement of the obvious. "Yeah." He did his shy smile. It had been almost a year since I'd seen it and I had forgotten how adorable it was. He ran his finger over the nick in his eyebrow and said, "A bunch of us are going off-roading. Would you like to come with us?"

I stared at him for an awkwardly long time. After I blinked three times, I finally forced myself to breathe and answered, "Can't. Have to work." My Neanderthal sentences came across sounding rude, so I scrambled to find more words. "Thanks anyway."

"What time do you get off?"

"Never. Um, I mean, it's not like a real job. It kind of depends on how busy it is. And it is. Busy. This weekend. Lots of people."

"Okay. Would you like to go to a party with me in Squamish

14

tonight?" His hand rose in a hold-on-a-second gesture. "Before you answer, I want to remind you about the deal we made last summer. Remember?"

I remembered our deal—of course I remembered our deal. I had thought about it about a thousand times since then—I was just surprised he remembered. The deal had happened during a crazy time in my life. I had just found out my boyfriend Steve had cheated on me. Trevor had just gotten home after five months away but made it clear we shouldn't be more than friends. And to top it all off Mason informed me that if we were both single when he got back from working abroad for a year, he would ask me out on a date. At the time, I didn't know where I would be living in a year or if Trevor and I would be together in a year. Plus, I had always been curious about Mason, so I had agreed. But I thought the chances of him actually honoring the deal were slim. Apparently I was wrong.

He seemed half-amused and half-worried by my lack of response. "What do you say?"

Again, I was frozen in an excruciatingly awkward stare as I considered the prospect of a summer fling with him. Then I choked out, "Sure."

"Great. I'll pick you up at eight." He handed me a business card. "Here's my number. Text me yours."

I nodded like a bobble head.

His mouth flashed a lopsided smile as if he wanted to laugh at my peculiar behaviour, but he hid it with the back of his hand, probably not wanting to be rude. I knew I was acting like an idiot, but tragically I couldn't help it. Mason was literally the best-looking human being I had ever met. To save my dignity, I didn't even attempt to say anything else. I just waved at him, then watched him run back through the rain and climb into the truck.

The guy in the passenger seat said something. Mason nodded, smiled, and then waved at me before he drove off with the convoy

15

of trucks following him south on the highway. I jiggled around, trying to contain my excitement.

"Is that a friend?" Granddad asked, making me jump out of my seat.

Clutching my chest to attempt to still my heartbeat, I said, "No. Not exactly. I kind of know him from school. He's one year older than I am. We never really hung out with the same crowds."

"Does he go to university?"

"No, he works for his dad's import business. He's been travelling, so I haven't seen him since last summer."

"What's his name?"

"Mason."

"The Cartwright boy?"

I glanced at him, curious that he'd heard of him. "Yes. Why?"

"No reason. Just wondering." Granddad didn't say anything else, but his eyebrows lifted and he nodded, as if he was impressed or something. He smiled, then wandered into the dining room, whistling.

Still not completely recovered from the shock, I picked up the phone and called Sophie. I was talking so fast and high-pitched only Sophie would have been able to decipher the content.

"Oh my God!" she said. "Why do all the good things happen while I'm not there? Okay, hold on. Cut it out, you idiots, I can't hear," she yelled at the guys in the van. "I need to focus. So, Mason Cartwright showed up at the Inn after a year abroad to honour your deal from that day at the Britannia pools last summer. And you have nothing to wear that even comes close to being suitable for a date with Mason Cartwright. Do I have it right so far?"

"Mmm hmm."

"Okay, calm down. Hold on. You guys, please shut up. This is an important call. Okay. This is huge. Does he still look good?"

"Unbelievably."

"Nice. What about Trevor?"

"What about Trevor? Could you please get over that? He has

16

a girlfriend. Oh, and more importantly, he doesn't share the same feelings. It's never going to happen. Mason is a real possibility."

"What if he's like all those pretentious snots he used to hang out with at school?"

"I don't know, but I should give him one chance, right?"

"Hell yeah. No girl in her right mind wouldn't go on at least one date with Mason Cartwright." Sophie laughed, then shouted away from the phone, "Oh, simmer down, Doug, I'm not a girl in her right mind." She switched back to me again, "I just don't know Mason well enough to be sure if he's a good guy."

"How will I be able to tell?"

"You'll feel it. Are you positive you don't want to hold out for Trevor? It's been a month since you saw him. Maybe you should at least wait to talk to him and see if he's going to make a move."

"I did talk to him. He called."

"And?"

"And nothing. Nothing has changed. Nothing will ever change. He asked me to save him a damn muffin. I've been holding out all year and now he's taken. I'm moving on."

"Hey, Doug. How do you think Trevor will feel about Deri hooking up with Mason Cartwright?" He made a grumbling sound. I couldn't make out his words, but he probably didn't want to get involved, since he was friends with both of us. Sophie laughed. "Yeah. That's what I thought. Tell him he blew it. Boys are so stupid. Damn. I wish I could be there to do your hair and makeup. This is so exciting. Okay, wear your new European jeans with the dark-purple halter-top and the black heels I lent you— yes, before you say anything, I did see every one of your posts from your trip, even though I said I didn't want to know how much fun you were having. It was obviously an awesome experi-ence. You looked amazing in that outfit. That is all I will say about that. We are never again talking about that opportunity of a lifetime I missed out on. Or just give me a week. I'll probably want to talk about it by then—next, under no circumstances may you wear your ugly faded cardigan. I don't care how rainy it is out. Straighten your hair and wear it parted in the middle. Mascara and lip gloss should be enough. You don't want to look like you're trying too hard. I want details first thing in the morning. Promise?"

"I promise. Thanks." I scribbled down some notes so I wouldn't forget her advice. "Good luck tonight."

"Get lucky tonight," she teased.

# CHAPTER 3

The afternoon dragged compared to the crazy morning. I was worried about Trevor getting hurt while he was training for Search and Rescue and jittery about the date with Mason. Despite checking the clock constantly, time didn't seem to be passing properly. Trevor hadn't replied to my text, so of course I assumed the worst and visualized all sorts of horrifying accidents that could leave him dead at the bottom of a ravine or river or something. I couldn't even concentrate enough to read the novel I was three-quarters through.

After finishing the orientation with Alan and Paula, Granddad took over the front-desk duties to give me a break. They hung out in the lobby with him to ask questions about things like the plumbing and furnace. Those weren't things I knew much about, but I agreed to meet Paula in the morning and walk her through the steps for getting the breakfast buffet ready. Their enthusiasm was cute.

Kailyn came over at three o'clock for our checkers game in the dining room. She beat me without me even letting her. "You're getting good, Kiki. Have you been practicing?"

"Trevor plays with me before I go to bed. He's bad. He always loses like you." As she set the board up for another game, I went into the kitchen to heat a homemade cinnamon bun for us to share. They were her favourite, along with my homemade hot chocolate. When I returned to the table with the tray, her mood shifted. She rocked back and forth in her chair and fidgeted with the checker pieces. "Derian, are you going to leave?"

I knew she wouldn't like the truth because change was not something she was comfortable with, but I couldn't lie to her, so I said, "A new family is moving in to run the Inn starting September. I'm probably going to move to Toronto to go to a school there. They are a really nice family. You'll like them."

"Toronto is far away. When will I see you?"

"During the holidays, I guess." Her expression was heartbreaking, so I added, "But there is also a small chance I might move to my mom's in Vancouver and go to Trevor's school. I haven't decided yet."

"You don't like your mom. You can live with us."

"What? Why would you say that? I like my mom." I frowned, wondering where she got that idea from. Obviously I'd given her that impression with all my complaining over the years. "Okay, I admit, my mom might be a little challenging for me to live with, but I love her. And thanks for the offer, but it's too inconvenient to drive from Britannia Beach to school every day."

"I don't want you to move away."

"I'm sorry, but I can't stay here forever."

She looked incredibly disappointed and I couldn't handle it. I dropped extra mini marshmallows into her hot chocolate, but she didn't take the mug when I offered it to her. She stared down at the tile pattern on the floor, still rocking. She had flip flops on and it looked as if she'd been hiking through mud puddles.

"Did you go into the forest?"

"No." She was a horrible liar. Her facial expression always gave her away.

"You're not supposed to go into the forest by yourself."

She tucked her feet under the table so I couldn't see them. "I'm a grown-up, Derian. I can do whatever I want."

"I know, but it's not safe to go in the forest by yourself."

She picked up the mug and sipped the hot chocolate in a delay tactic. "I didn't."

"Really? How did your feet get so dirty?"

She leaned forward and rested her elbows on the table. "Don't tell Trevor. He'll be mad."

"He won't be mad. He just doesn't want you to get lost. Your dad and Trevor were really scared that time you got lost in the forest."

"I won't get lost again. I promise."

"Okay. Good." A man I didn't recognize entered the Inn, and Granddad was showing Paula and Alan something in the basement, so I got up and rushed over to scoot behind the front desk and help the man. He had reddish-blond hair that was thin on top. His small eyes flicked around, searching for something. His gaze never rested on me even when I asked, "May I help you?"

"I need a room until next Wednesday."

"Okay. We only have one small one left and it's on the highway side."

"That's fine." He nodded. "I'll take whatever you have. Everything in Squamish is full."

"Oh yeah, there is a big baseball tournament going on. They're usually booked a year in advance for that. I'm going to need a credit card and a piece of picture ID," I said.

He frowned and sighed in a tense, irritated way. "I don't have a credit card. I'll pay cash up front."

"There's a damage deposit of two hundred dollars. You'll get it back when you check out if the room is in the same condition you found it in."

"Fine," he said and opened his wallet. A credit card was perfectly visible in the first slot. When he realized I had noticed it, he tipped his wallet until I couldn't see the card.

I told him how much he owed and he counted out the entire amount in one-hundred-dollar bills. While I was getting the key, I caught him staring at Kailyn through the archway to the dining room. He was already creeping me out, but when he focused on Kailyn like that I felt extremely uncomfortable. "I'm going to need a copy of your driver's licence in case you leave anything behind in the room." I totally lied, but I wanted to have a record of him just in case.

"It's in my suitcase," he said, even though he didn't have a suitcase with him. "I'll bring it down later this evening."

He was a quick liar, which made me more wary. "Your room is up the stairs and on the right. A buffet breakfast is available in the dining room between six and nine," I said as he walked away. He didn't say thanks.

Kailyn had kept playing while I was gone, so I had almost no checkers left. "Did you see that man?" I whispered.

"Yes. Is he a bad man?"

"I don't know for sure. It would be better if you didn't talk to him or go anywhere with him just in case. Okay?"

"Okay." She cleared the board and set it up to play again. "Do you think I'll ever meet Riley Rivers?"

"Sure," I said, but I was distracted because Murphy's light-green GMC pulled into the parking lot with Trevor in the passenger seat. He looked as if he was still in one piece. It was a relief, but it meant something bad was still going to happen to someone at some point. Trevor transferred his climbing gear back into his own truck. Murphy waved one of his massive arms out the window, then drove away. Kailyn noticed me staring, so she followed my gaze.

"Trevor's home." She got up, grabbed her half of the cinnamon bun to take with her, and walked out without saying goodbye to me.

I cleaned up the game and returned it to the library, then loitered around the lobby, waiting to see if Trevor was going to come by and tell me about his trip. He didn't call or come over, so I decided to focus on getting ready for my date with Mason instead.

Sophie's instructions were extremely helpful, and although I didn't come close to resembling the girls who used to hang out with Mason in high school, I looked pretty good for me. Sophie's heels made my legs look even longer, which I liked, because my legs were my best feature. And thanks to the conditioner I had brought back from Italy, my hair turned out extra shiny and smooth. A cardigan would have been my first choice, since it was still raining torrentially, but Sophie was right, it made the whole outfit look dumpy. For the sake of fashion I committed to braving the weather with bare arms.

When I was finally as presentable as possible without professional help, I headed to the lobby. Trevor was leaning his elbows on the front desk and laughing with my granddad. He had on a white dress shirt, dark jeans, and motorcycle boots. He smelled really good. They both saw me at the same time. My granddad whistled, which made me feel suddenly very self-conscious. Trevor stood up straight and stared at me without saying anything. His expression was weird. I looked down at myself to see if I had screwed something up. The clothes seemed to look okay, so I smoothed my hair with my hands to check if it had gone awry. It seemed okay too. I stared back at Trevor and tried to figure out why he wasn't smiling.

Granddad excused himself, smiling and mumbling something I couldn't quite hear as he disappeared through the archway into the dining room.

"Welcome home." Trevor finally said as he stepped closer to give me a quick, friendly hug. "You look really pretty, Deri."

"Thanks." I tucked my hair behind my ears and glanced down at the floor. "I did the best I could without Sophie's help. You look nice, too. Are you going on a date?"

"Uh, no. I'm just meeting up with Murphy and the guys later. Do you want me to give you a ride somewhere?"

"Oh, no thanks. Mason is picking me up."

"Mason," Trevor said and frowned as he glanced out the window.

"Do you remember him?"

"Yeah." He looked at me briefly and then focused somewhere off in the distance, thinking. "I thought he moved away."

"Sort of. Not really. He was just travelling abroad for work."

"Oh."

An unusually sleek silver sports car pulled up in front of the Inn. Mason got out of the car and Granddad came back into the lobby as if he'd been waiting around the corner, listening. Mason opened the front door and said hello to me, then shook hands with Granddad as he introduced himself. He made eye contact with Trevor, who was standing beside me. He lifted his chin in a guy nod, and said, "Maverty."

"Cartwright." Trevor did the guy nod back.

There was a bit of an awkward silence before Granddad told us to have a good time and excused himself. It was pouring out, so I moved next to the door and waited for Mason.

"Keep that McLaren close to the speed limit," Trevor told Mason. "She gets uncomfortable driving on the highway."

Mason nodded, then ran out into the rain to open the passenger door for me. Trevor didn't look impressed that Mason was my date, but he really had no right to have an opinion. "I don't need you to tell him how to drive. You're not my dad."

"Be safe." His voice was genuine, and it made me feel guilty for snapping at him.

I pushed my palm against the front door, then hesitated. "The muffin I saved for you is in the Tupperware container on the counter in the kitchen." I swung the door open and ran out into the storm.

Mason's car wasn't like any car I'd ever seen before. The vertical air vents on the side looked like shark gills and the door opened upwards instead of to the side. I slid down into the leather seats.

It felt like I was getting into the cockpit of a fighter jet or the Batmobile. Mason ran around the back, opened his door, and slid in behind the steering wheel. He turned the heat up and the music down. "You look beautiful," he said.

"Thanks, you do, too. I mean not beautiful—handsome, or good. You look nice," I finally spat out. He had on a long-sleeved, charcoal-coloured, V-neck shirt and dark dress pants. He did look nice, classy, like the guys in Europe. I glanced back at the window to the lobby. Trevor was gone. He must have left through the kitchen. "What's a McLaren?" I asked.

Mason smiled and said, "It's just a fast car. Trevor ruined all the fun, though. I'll have to show you what it can do someday when the weather's better, which is okay with me because it guarantees a second date."

I did suddenly feel nervous, but it had nothing to do with driving too fast. We hadn't even left the parking lot.

# CHAPTER 4

Mason drove a little faster than the speed limit, but it didn't bother me because his car handled smoothly and clung to the curves of the highway. He kept looking at me, probably to make sure I wasn't going to have a meltdown on him.

Eventually, he cleared his throat and said, "Uh, I heard you weren't dating anyone right now, but if that's not the case I—"

"I'm single."

"So, there's nothing going on between you and Trevor?"

"No."

He glanced at me briefly before focusing back on the road. "I don't want to get in the middle of anything."

"Don't worry. You're not."

He nodded but didn't seem entirely convinced. "He said you're uncomfortable driving on the highway. Does that have something to do with how your dad died?"

I took in a deep breath and stared out the side window at the rock face passing by, trying to decide how much I wanted to share with him. I took another breath and said, "Yeah. The car accident happened about a kilometre away from the Inn."

Mason's eyebrows angled with concern. Although it had gotten a little easier over the years to tell people about my dad, it was still painful to go into details about the accident, so I mastered avoidance techniques.

"Anyway, I just get a little weird about driving fast on the highway. Sorry."

"Don't be sorry. It's understandable." He eased the pressure off the accelerator and we slowed to the speed limit.

Neither of us spoke, and it made me hyper-aware of everything—the tremble in my hands, how loud I was breathing, how little I actually knew about him. To distract myself from the anxious thinking that was inevitably going to snowball, I racked my brain for something to talk about. Anything. "So, where have you been travelling for the last year?"

"Pretty much everywhere—Milan, Amsterdam, Istanbul, Tokyo, Berlin, London, Paris, and New York. My dad threw me into the deep end to see if I would sink or swim."

"And?"

He laughed. "I'm doing more of a dog paddle, but he hasn't fired me yet."

"What do you do, exactly?"

"Basically, I find out what other people are willing to pay a lot of money for and get it for them."

"Sounds interesting."

"Not really. I'm either on an airplane, in meetings, or on the phone in a hotel room most of the time."

I turned in the seat to face him. "You've been living out of hotels for a year?"

"You make it sound horrible." He pointed at me to tease. "You technically live in a hotel."

"Right." I chuckled and shrugged to concede the point. "I guess it's not so bad. Will you always have to travel that much?"

"For a while, but once I learn about every part of the business, I'll probably just go on a couple of big trips a year. That's what my dad does now." He down-shifted through the curves in the road and the engine rumbled. I really wasn't into fancy things, but it was undeniably an impressive car.

"Did your dad travel a lot when you were growing up?"

"Yeah. He was gone most of the time. One time, when I was about four, he tried to hug me after he'd been away for two months and I cried because I thought he was a stranger." He chuckled, but there was something else in the tone of his voice that made it seem like it was a painful memory. "My mom likes to tell everyone that story. It's her way of complaining that he wasn't around."

"Are you closer to your dad now that you work together?"

"It's getting better." He nodded pensively. "I think I've figured out how to impress him."

"Has he figured out how to impress you?"

Mason licked his bottom lip and seemed uncomfortable with the question. He finally said, "I don't know," and accelerated to pass a row of slow-moving cars. The engine revved as we sped effortlessly along the twists of the highway. Once we had left the other traffic behind, the engine quieted and we slowed down. "Sorry," he said.

At first I wondered why he apologized but then I realized I'd had my eyes clenched shut and my fingers clamping my knees. "Oh. No. I'm fine." I relaxed and exhaled. "Actually, I'm sorry. I shouldn't have asked such personal questions about your dad. We hardly know each other."

"Personal is good. You can ask me whatever you want. Seriously, I'm so tired of shallow conversations and superficial people. Tell me more about your dad. You must miss him."

I nodded and sighed. "I do. Desperately. We were very close and I would do anything to have just one more day with him. You're lucky you and your dad still have the opportunity to grow even closer."

He concentrated on the winding road, gripping the steering wheel tightly. Even though he said he was okay with the deeper, personal conversation, he really didn't seem to be. Eventually he asked, "What was it like to grow up in Britannia Beach?"

"Life in a tiny roadside village is not fascinating enough to be considered a conversation topic I don't think."

"Try me. Tell me something you used to do as a kid."

"Um, let's see." I skipped over most of my good memories because they all included Trevor. I definitely didn't want to go on about him to Mason. It took a while, but I eventually came up with one. "On hot summer days I used to set up a lemonade stand in the parking lot in front of the Inn. I made so much money from tourists going by on the highway that my dad opened up a bank account for me. I still have all the money. It's part of my university fund."

"How entrepreneurial of you."

I gestured to showcase the features of his car. "Well, I didn't make quite enough to afford a luxury McLaren."

He laughed. "Neither did I. My dad gave me the car." His eyes shifted sideways and met my gaze. "I think I would like to spend more time in Britannia Beach."

"I'm pretty sure you'll be begging for an airplane and a hotel room in a foreign country after a couple of hours."

"Not if you're here."

I shoved his shoulder playfully. "Well, although that is obviously your attempt to be funny, I'm only going to be here for the rest of the summer."

He shook his head. "I wasn't trying to be funny."

I rolled my eyes, but when his expression remained serious I realized he wasn't joking. Not sure what to think of that, I tucked my hair behind my ears and focused on the scenery. We had already arrived in Squamish. A few minutes later, we pulled up in front of a two-storey house made of glass and cedar posts arranged in sharp, clean angles. It was an homage to a Fred Hollingsworth design that I had driven past to admire before. Mason pulled into the roundabout driveway and stopped in front of the house. He got out of the car and rushed around to flip my door up for me. Then he offered his hand to help me step out. "You can wait in the house out of the rain while I park the car. I'll only be a minute."

I ran to stand under the overhang by the front door and wrapped my bare arms around my body. I didn't want to go inside because I didn't even know whose house it was. Three girls who went to my school in Mason's graduating class filed out of a cab and stumbled up the stone pathway towards the house. I smiled uncomfortably, hoping they would just walk by and ignore me. One of the girls, named Paige, smiled back, but the other two glared at me. The one named Corrine Andrews curled her lip up as if I was dirty or disgusting in some way. They went into the house without knocking and slammed the door shut behind them. They must have been drunk because they were way too loud and I could hear them through the door. "Who is that?"

"Isn't she Trevor Maverty's sister?"

"I thought his sister has Down syndrome?"

"Not that one. The sister who works at the Britannia Beach Inn."

"Trevor only has one sister. The girl who works at the Inn is Derian Lafleur. Remember her? She hangs out with that vampire chick in your cousin's band."

"Oh yeah, I remember. That girl outside wasn't Derian. Derian isn't that pretty."

Mason jogged towards me. He was soaking wet, but smiling. Obviously, my face was still locked in the same expression it had been while I was eavesdropping on the girls through the door because his smile faded. "What's wrong?"

"Nothing," I forced myself to be animated and sound convincing. "I think I'm just a little nervous to meet your friends."

"They're not so bad. I'll protect you," he joked as he squeezed his arm across my shoulders and led me into the house.

My palms got sweaty.

# CHAPTER 5

The three girls were still in the foyer, fixing their hair and makeup in the mirror. They turned to see Mason with me and all of their mouths dropped open. Any sliver of confidence I did have, drained out of me when I took a closer look at how they were dressed. Pedicures, strappy high heels, shiny tanned skin, silky dresses that most people would have considered more of a blouse, and diamonds decorating their fingers, wrists, necks, and ears. They almost reeked of money. I reeked of a one-hundred-year-old Inn off the highway. A pair of jeans from London weren't quite enough to catapult me into their league.

Mason didn't seem to notice all the reeking as he introduced me. Paige smiled again. The second girl didn't smile, but she offered a limp handshake. Corrine literally squished her nose up and turned back towards the mirror without even saying hello. "Corrine," Mason said, obviously irritated by her rudeness.

She turned back to face Mason and produced the fakest smile. "Welcome home, Chancey. I've missed you." She leaned forward and kissed him on the lips.

He pulled his head back and frowned at her.

"Who's your new friend?"

"Derian. She went to school with us."

She glanced at me and added, "Oh, Derian. I remember. She's the maid at that little old Inn off the highway. I just didn't recognize her without her scruffy clothes on."

Mason glared at Corrine and took my hand. He escorted me away from them and into a living room that overlooked the ocean. "Sorry about that. It's not about you. She's just jealous because back in high school she wanted to date and I didn't."

I tucked my hair behind my ears and bit at my lower lip.

"You're uncomfortable. I'm sorry. Come on, I'll introduce you to some of my guy friends." He winked. "They shouldn't be quite as bitchy."

I smiled because he was cute, and I appreciated that he was trying, but I didn't feel good about being there. It wasn't like the parties I usually attended. I was used to Sophie and the band acting wild and playing way too loud until the party got broken up by the cops. I could barely even hear the music on the sound system in the background as Mason and I reached a crowd of guys who were ordering mixed drinks from an actual bartender in a white shirt and black vest.

A guy I recognized from school shouted, "Chancey!" and raised his glass to toast the air.

The four other guys who were standing with their backs to us turned around. They didn't look at Mason, they all ogled me instead. They nodded and made various comments like, "Way to go, Chance", "Nice work, Chancey", and "The infamous Chance Cartwright is back from his world tour and already on to his next conquest," as if I wasn't standing right there.

I tore my hand out of Mason's grasp and stormed back towards the door. I didn't know how I was going to get back to Britannia Beach, but I didn't really care. I was angry at myself for being stupid enough to fall for his lines. He had dated a lot of girls in high school and I had been warned back then that he had a reputation for one-night stands. At the time I never put much stock in the exaggerated rumours because my instincts had always given me the sense that there was more depth to him than the rumours gave him credit for. Apparently I was wrong. It was blatantly obvious I was just another piece of ass to him.

Mason caught up with me and pulled my elbow to make me turn and look at him. "Derian, I'm sorry. I didn't know they were going to be assholes. I overestimated them."

Once my awe-struck impression of him was shattered, my more assertive side surfaced. I didn't care what he thought about me anymore. Frustrated, I poked my index finger into his chest. "I'm not some dumb slut who is dying to say I was with Mason Cartwright. You're not that impressive to me."

He reeled back. I couldn't tell if he was hurt or mad. "Please don't let my *ex* friends taint your opinion of me."

"Why? It's hard not to assume you're at least a little like them. You must have something in common with them. And presumably they know you well enough to have a pretty good idea about what your intentions with me were. Are there really women out there who let your friends talk about them like that?"

He didn't have a response. He turned his head to the side, clenched his jaw, and closed his eyes in a long blink. His expressions were really hard to read and I had no idea what he was feeling. I didn't plan to stick around to find out.

"This was a mistake," I said as I fumbled through my purse, looking for my phone.

"No, Derian, don't say that." He reached forward and held both my wrists so I wouldn't dial my phone. "Please, let me prove to you I'm not like them." He stared into my eyes and waited for me to say something.

Disappointed that he wasn't the sophisticated and interesting person I had hoped he was, I asked, "Why do they call you Chance? Is that some sort of womanizer thing?"

"It's stupid and immature." He dropped his hands. "And it's not true. Let me finish our date so you can form your own opinions. Please."

My instincts were still telling me there was more to him than rumours and reputation, but the glaring evidence to the contrary was making it difficult to know for sure. I studied him without saying anything, trying to detect a sign in his expression that would confirm he was bullshitting. "Why would I bother wasting my time on a date with a guy who only wants one thing? One thing he's not going to get, by the way."

"It's not like that. I just want you to get to know me better. Nothing more." His tone actually sounded genuine. In fact, he appeared to be upset about what was happening.

I leaned back against the wall and crossed my arms. "You invited me here to meet your friends as a way to get to know you better, but you are allegedly nothing like your friends, so how does that help me gain an accurate impression?"

He tilted his head back and exhaled tension. "It doesn't. I don't know what I was thinking."

"Did you ask me out only because you want to sleep with me?"

"No. I mean, maybe one day, but no. I just wanted you to get to know me better."

"Why?"

He chuckled like it was a stupid question. "Because I like you."

"Why?" I challenged.

"What do you mean why? I like you because you're smart and gorgeous and nice to everyone. And even though I've been gone for a year, I never stopped wondering about you."

It didn't make sense. Guys like him who could date and sleep with whomever they wanted didn't wait around a year for small-town girls like me. Something didn't fit. "Why? It's not like you knew me that well before you left."

"I know we didn't spend any time together in high school, but I always noticed you. You sketch buildings when you're bored; you smile at the people most other people ignore; you laugh out loud when something is only a little funny, and you laugh silently when something is really funny; your cheeks go red if someone compliments you and you believe them, but not if you think they're being fake; and you don't lie about who you are because you don't need to. Everyone else was phony and had an agenda for being my friend. But not you. Your genuineness stuck out right from the first time I saw you. And, honestly, I liked the fact that you were one of the few girls who didn't throw yourself at me because of my dad's money."

My eyes darted back and forth between his face and the party in the background as my mind attempted to process everything. It was nice to know that he had noticed me back then. I had definitely noticed him, too. But I was still worried I was nothing more than a hard-to-get conquest in a game that had gotten too easy for him.

Sensing that I was undecided, he smiled tentatively and wrapped his arm around my waist. "Come on. Let's go upstairs where we can be alone. I want to show you something."

"You're joking, right?" I shoved his arm off me.

"No. I didn't mean—it's not like that. Shit, this is getting worse by the minute," he said under his breath.

With one hand propped on my hip and a snarky tone, I said, "Sorry to ruin your night."

"It's not you. I'm messing everything up. It's my fault and I just want to make it better. Tell me how to make it better."

"Take me home."

"I don't want to take you home." He stared at me, struggling to think of something to say that would change my mind. "The party was a bad idea. I should have taken you on a proper date. We can go somewhere else, just the two of us. Tell me where you want to go."

I shook my head without saying anything. Going somewhere else wasn't going to change the fact that we were from completely different worlds and had nothing in common. And it wouldn't change the fact that he had only one goal, which despite Sophie's encouragement to be more adventurous, was not a goal I shared.

After a long silence, he sighed and his perfect posture sunk slightly. "If you want to go home, I'll take you home, but I've really been looking forward to tonight. I don't want it to end before it even starts."

I had never met anyone who was so hard to read. His face only showed his feelings part of the time, in flashes. It was like putting the pieces of a puzzle together, only most of the pieces were missing.

"Why does this mean so much to you?" I asked.

His eyebrows angled together and he checked over his shoulder to make sure nobody was close enough to hear our conversation. "When I moved to Squamish and saw you around school, it was obvious there was something different and special about you—not just because you're pretty, nice, and smart. It's hard to explain, but it felt like you could see me. Not like everyone else saw me, but for who I really am. Being the new kid at school for senior year, it was easier to let people like me for my image and reputation. It felt nice to know that at least one person knew there was more to me than that. I was intrigued that you noticed that side of me even without ever having a conversation with me. I'm not only telling you this to flatter you, but nobody has ever made me feel the way you do when you look at me. I know it sounds weird because we haven't spent any time together. But that's why I'm interested in getting to know you better. And that's why I've been looking forward to finally spending time with you. I'm sorry I got too excited and didn't put enough thought into planning the actual date. I haven't even talked to most of these people in a year."

It took a while for everything he said to filter through my brain. It was quite the speech and I knew the connection he was referring to. I had always felt like I saw a different Mason than everyone else saw. I glanced around at the people at the party— people who thought they knew him because of the type of clothes

36

he wore and the type of cars he drove. It was sad to imagine what it was like to be friends with people who didn't really know you. "Maybe you need to make some new friends who take the time to appreciate the real you," I said.

He lifted his gaze to make direct eye contact with me. "I'm working on it."

I nodded and then sighed as I thought. He waited patiently as I considered all the options. Anyone watching us would have probably assumed he was being really smooth and I was being naïve, but for some reason that I couldn't exactly explain, I knew without a doubt there was more to him and that he was willing to share it with me if I let him. And I wanted to let him. "What did you want to show me upstairs?"

He flashed an appreciative grin and took my hand again. "It's a surprise. You'll like it." He led me up a staircase that floated on suspension wires. At the top, a glass door opened out onto a rooftop deck. It would have had a 360-degree view of the ocean and the mountains if it weren't for the low, heavy clouds. We ran through the rain towards the front ledge of the deck and ducked into a cedar gazebo to stay dry. He sat on the bench and I slid down beside him to look at the spectacular view.

He was right when he assumed I would like it. And, although it was cold out, being isolated from the rest of the party made me way more comfortable. "The city lights are beautiful," I said.

He pointed further down the coastline to a tiny cluster of lights off by themselves. "Can you see the Inn?"

"Oh yeah. It looks so tiny." I shivered from the cold and folded my hands in my lap. "My granddad sold it."

"I heard. How do feel about that?"

"Not great, but he's ready to retire."

"Why doesn't your mom live at the Inn?"

"She works at a law firm in Vancouver. We have an apartment down there. She used to visit on weekends when I was a kid, but she doesn't come up much since my dad died. She's phobic about driving on the highway." I inhaled and changed the subject, "What is your favourite city?"

"New York."

"I'm jealous you've been there. I can only imagine what it must be like. I would love to see the architecture in real life someday."

He nodded. "Every self-respecting architect needs to visit the Guggenheim. We should definitely do something about that."

I glanced at him, hoping he didn't mean he wanted to take me there. I wasn't sure how he even knew I was planning to study architecture. If I had told him, it meant he remembered it for more than a year. "Maybe offering trips to New York was what you had to do to impress your old friends, but people like me don't need grand gestures to decide if we like a person or not."

He reached into his pocket and pulled out a jewellery box. "Would you be opposed to a small gesture?"

"Mason. You didn't need to buy me anything."

"Sorry. I'm used to showing appreciation with gifts." He lifted the lid. Inside was a necklace with a very small, blue, enamelled, flower pendant. "It's hand made," he added as he searched my face to see if I liked it.

"Wow. It's beautiful and so unique."

"Like you," he said.

My face flared up in what probably looked like scarlet blotches. Fortunately, it was too dark for him to notice. It was very strange and overwhelming to hear a guy talk like he was totally into me when we had barely even started our first date. It was probably his game. But it didn't feel like he was playing me. However, that's likely what all girls who've been played believe. I didn't know what to think. "It must have been very expensive. I can't accept it."

"You have to. I bought it in Paris when I was there last month, so I can't return it."

"You were in Paris last month? Really? I was there three weeks

38

ago. That would have been so surreal to run into each other there."

He slid the chain over my collarbone and I gathered my hair over one shoulder so he could clasp it at the back. Money was obviously not a big deal to him, but it made me feel weird to accept such a lavish gift on a first date. His intentions were sweet, though, so I reluctantly accepted it.

"Thank you."

"You're welcome." He ran the back of his hand down my arm, which sent goose bumps shooting across the surface. "You're cold. We should go back inside."

"No, it's only goose bumps. I'm okay. This is nice, just the two of us. Let's stay here and talk a little longer."

He agreed and pulled me close to wrap his arm around my shoulder. "Where are you going to school in the fall?" he asked.

"University of Toronto. I think. Do you regret not going to school?"

"Yes and no. I was going to end up working for my dad anyway, so in some ways there was no point in delaying a guaranteed career. In other ways, I sometimes wish I could have decided my career path on my own."

"What subject interests you?"

He chuckled a little and glanced at me. "Marine biology."

"Why is that funny?"

"It's not. It's just that nobody's ever asked me before. Everyone always assumes I would want to make a fortune working for my dad."

"Does working for your dad make you happy?"

His eyebrows angled together in a deep crease again. "I guess. It depends on your definition of happy."

"Free to be yourself, feeling safe, important and loved, being passionate about what you do, and making the people you care about smile."

"Wow. You've obviously thought about that one before."

"Not really. I just know what makes me happy. Don't you know?"

He appeared to get lost in his thoughts as he looked out over the stormy water. His face was essentially perfect except for the small scar that cut through his right eyebrow. It honestly felt a little bizarre to sit so close to him since all the other times I'd ever admired him were only ever from a distance. He turned to me and said, "I'm happy right now. I know that much."

I smiled. "You say very provocative things, Mr. Cartwright."

"Provocative is good, right?"

I laughed. "I haven't quite figured that out yet, but I'm curious to find out."

"Curious is good." He raised his eyebrows, pleased with the glimmer of hope. "You must be getting cold. Do you want to get out of here and go somewhere for dessert or something?"

I wasn't looking forward to making our way through his so-called friends again, but it was unpleasantly cold and we couldn't hide out on the roof all night, so I agreed. We dashed back through the rain across the rooftop and got soaked. As we walked hand in hand down the suspended staircase, I scanned the room, making note of the unfriendly faces so we could avoid them. Corrine was across the room, flirting with a guy who was seated on the arm of a couch with his back to me. The muscles of his shoulders pulled his shirt tight and I knew who he was without even seeing his face. Corrine laughed and flipped her head to the side to make her long platinum hair cascade over her shoulder. She spotted Mason and me and her expression transitioned into a snotty sneer.

Beyond Corrine I noticed Murphy's shaved head. He was seated on the chair opposite the couch. He nodded towards me to make Trevor turn around. As soon as he made eye contact with me, Trevor's entire frame tensed and he rose to his feet. The expression on his face was the same one he got whenever someone teased or hurt Kailyn. *Shit.* I touched my cheek and remembered that the rain probably made me look battered from the smeared mascara. "Mason, does it look like I was crying?"

He smiled. "Kind of. Do you want to go to the washroom and freshen up?"

"It's too late," I whispered as Trevor took long strides towards us.

# CHAPTER 6

Trevor stopped directly in front of Mason. They were almost the same height and stood chest to chest. Trevor scanned my face more closely, then turned towards Mason and glared at him. Rage flickered through Trevor's eyes and Mason let my hand drop.

"Did he hurt you?" Trevor asked me without taking his eyes off Mason.

"No! I'm fine," I insisted and pressed my hand against Trevor's bicep to hold him back.

"Did you make her cry?" Trevor spoke really slowly through clenched teeth, trying to restrain himself.

"No," I answered for him as I squished myself in between the two of them. My body wedged up against Trevor's to push him back. Using all my strength made no difference. He didn't move at all. Murphy and a couple of other guys stood on alert a few feet away. "I'm fine," I said again.

Trevor's eyebrows angled together as he checked my expression, probably to see if I was lying to save Mason's ass.

I held my breath and scrambled for a way to defuse the situation. "It's raining. My mascara ran. Can we drop it, please? You're making a scene."

Trevor must have believed me because he glared at Mason one

more time, then stepped back and relaxed his muscles. "Your clothes are wet. Come on, I'll take you home."

"If she wants to go home, I can take her home," Mason said.

They both faced me, waiting for me to tell them what I wanted to do. The night hadn't gone well right from the start. I was drenched. And everyone was staring. Since Trevor lived next door, I said, "It's okay, Mason. I don't want you to have to drive all the way back and forth again in this weather. Trevor's going that way anyway."

It was obvious by his expression that Mason didn't want to end our date that way, but it didn't make sense for him to drive back and forth to Britannia Beach again when he didn't have to. He reluctantly agreed and Trevor left to get the 4Runner.

Mason stood with me in the foyer as I waited. He leaned his back against the wall and shoved his hands in his pockets. "Sorry this didn't go that well."

I shook my head to ease his concern. "Don't worry about it. It was nice to see you again and get to know you better. I think everyone deserves friends who like them for who they really are and I'm happy to be your friend. Thanks for everything."

Trevor pulled up in front of the house, so I said good-bye, gave Mason a quick hug, then I ran out through the rain and climbed into the truck.

"Are you honestly okay?" Trevor asked again. He looked at me in a way that made it seem like if I fessed up he would go back inside and take care of it.

"Yes. Let it go." I shut the door, then looked back at the house. Mason stood in the open doorway with his hands in his pockets but waved as we pulled away.

Trevor and I drove in silence. He didn't have the radio on, so the rain sounded loud as it hit the roof and sprayed off the pavement up into the wheel wells. I glanced at him. His jaw was tense and the serious angles of his face made him look older.

"I wasn't crying," I said. "We went out on the rooftop deck in the rain to avoid everyone because Corrine said something really snotty about me being a maid and all the guys there acted as if I was just fresh meat."

"Corrine's a bitch and you are fresh meat to those guys."

"Really?" I scoffed. "You didn't seem to think Corrine was a bitch when she was all up on you."

"Whoa. Jealous?"

"No. Why would I be jealous? I was on a date with a really interesting guy."

His jaw muscle twitched. "I don't like him."

"Well, your opinion of him is completely irrelevant. I can date whomever I want to date. I don't need your approval." I reached over and turned the radio on.

Trevor immediately turned it off again. "He's going to hurt you."

I shook my head, so tired of the same old pattern repeating with us. "I'm not a little kid anymore. When you moved off to college, I grew up. I am perfectly capable of thinking for myself and taking care of myself. He's a nice guy. You don't even know him."

"I know guys like him."

"Yeah? Who cares?" I snapped. "It's not like it even matters who I date. I'm moving away at the end of the summer."

He glanced at me, but instead of responding, he turned the radio back on. God. He was so aggravating. He knew I had feelings for him in the past. He knew he would have been my first choice. I wouldn't have even considered Toronto if he had given me any indication there was hope for us to be together after high school. But he hadn't. The fact that he had blocked every attempt I ever made to be with him gave him no right to block my other options. I dropped the argument and stared out the window, arms crossed, face scowled. Tension vibrated off him, which only made me more furious because it was none of his business.

When we were halfway home a déjà vu feeling crashed over

me. My heart rate accelerated. I sat up as I recognized flashes from my vision: the dark, the rain, the road. It all looked familiar.

"Trevor, stop the truck. Stop! Stop! Stop!" I screamed and braced my hands against the dashboard.

# CHAPTER 7

Trevor slammed on the brakes and locked his arms against the steering wheel as the truck fish-tailed and then skidded to a stop. We both gawked out the windshield at the gaping blackness that stretched out in front of the headlights. Trevor threw the truck into reverse and pulled it to the shoulder of the highway. "Call 911 and tell them the bridge is washed out in both directions."

He jumped out and ran to open the back of the canopy. Grabbing my phone, I got out of the truck and rushed towards the edge, where the highway disappeared into nothing. We had been only inches from plummeting to the rocks below. I told the dispatcher what happened as Trevor lit a bunch of fluorescent-red road flares and spread them across the highway behind us. He lit more and tossed them over the gap to warn any drivers approaching from the other direction.

The operator was still asking me questions as I stared out where the highway used to be. My vision had saved us. The stream was a raging river of rapids bulging high on the banks. Some of the ruins of what used to be the cement bridge were wedged in a contorted heap up against the boulders. Part of the bridge still hung precariously and the metal rebar ground as it buckled under the pressure of the rumbling water. It made a hideous sound.

Underneath the water was a bluish glow. Dread flooded my bloodstream when I realized what it was. I shouted and probably startled the operator. "Trevor! There's a car in the water. I can see the headlights."

Trevor stood at my side and peered over the edge. Without even hesitating, he ran back and got ropes, a helmet, and a life vest out of the truck. "Move the truck so the flood lights shine down on the water," he instructed me as he tore off his shirt and put the vest on.

He disappeared down into the black hole. He was so calm and technical. I was the opposite. I was panicked and struggling to keep it together as I moved the truck and tilted the floodlight towards the car that was half submerged in the water. If the driver survived the car crashing over the edge, the occupants were in danger of drowning. I kicked off Sophie's heels and, even though the operator told me to stay on the line, I tossed the phone on the front seat. The sharp edges of the rocks sliced at my bare feet as I scrambled down to the edge of the water. I didn't know what I was going to do to help. I just felt compelled to attempt something. Trevor set up his ropes and waded waist deep in the water, fighting the current to get close to the car. The driver hung limply from the seatbelt, but thankfully her head wasn't underwater.

I stepped ankle deep into the glacier-fed water, regretted it immediately, and hopped back out. Trevor wouldn't be able to stay in it for very long. He freed the woman from her seatbelt, but struggled against the pressure of the water to pull her out through the window. The mangled part of the bridge that was still partly attached shifted again. It made a demon screeching sound as huge chunks of cement fell into the water next to the car. Trevor glanced up at the bridge to check if there were more chunks about to fall, then he turned downstream to move diagonally with the current.

He pulled the woman's body through the water with his arms wrapped under her armpits and around her chest. It didn't seem like that much time had passed, but it must have because more floodlights angled down on us from the highway. The silhouette of two cops appeared on the ridge, then they climbed down the rocky bank towards me. One of the cops touched my arm as he passed me and asked, "Are you okay?"

I nodded, but his touch triggered a vision: I was in the back seat of the car. The woman smiled over her shoulder at me. She was singing. There was a toy in my hand and my little feet bounced with excitement. I was a toddler strapped into a car seat.

My vision ended and I screamed at Trevor, "There's a baby in the back seat! There's a baby."

Trevor passed the limp woman to one of the cops on shore and glanced at me with complete trust before he swam back through the water towards the car. It spun a quarter turn and wedged up against a boulder. The back seat became submerged. I gasped when Trevor took off his life vest to dive down. The bridge shifted again. Metal started popping out and bending as the water pulled on the foundation. I suddenly regretted telling Trevor what I'd seen in my vision. I hyperventilated as I realized my vision might have been wrong. It was so stupid of me to say anything.

I watched the surface of the water and waited for Trevor to come back up. It seemed like minutes passed and I still couldn't see him. More rescue people stumbled down the rocks with more equipment and they moved around in an organized way. After a deafening groan, the rest of the bridge broke free. It plummeted into the water with a thunderous splash. The impact shook the ground. The current caught the huge blocks of cement debris and collided with the car, making it spin sideways. The ropes Trevor had set up strained and twisted as the car dropped into deeper water and entirely disappeared.

One of the cops shouted, "Maverty's still in the car. Someone get in there quick."

Not wasting a second, I quickly waded in chest deep. The cold sucked the breath out of my lungs, but I had to get to where Trevor was trapped. The current was too swift to swim, so I fought against the pressure and stepped along the rocky bottom, following his guide lines, slipping and stumbling. Only the glow of the headlights was visible beneath the rapids. The stream got too deep and I had no choice but to lift my feet and propel myself towards the car.

My hand hit the roof first, then I reached forward and felt the glass of the window. I held my breath and dipped under the water. Trevor passed the tiny body of the toddler to me out the window. Not knowing what I was supposed to do, I quickly popped my head back up and rolled onto my back to keep the toddler's mouth above water, as much as possible. A torrent of water surged, spun me around, and pushed me below the surface again. Disoriented and terrified, I clung with one arm around the child and flailed my other arm to grasp onto the rocks that my back smashed against. I was only able to lift my head high enough to steal one gulp of air before the current tumbled me around again. On the second attempt, I was able to reach for an overhanging tree branch and cling to it. I pulled the toddler up over my shoulder. He wasn't moving. Trevor wasn't anywhere I could see. I wasn't even sure if he'd gotten out of the car. The headlights weren't visible anymore.

Silhouetted by the rescue floodlights, a massive bald man bounded down the rocky beach. It was Murphy. Instead of jumping into the water to save Trevor, he ran towards me. "Derian!" he gasped as he shimmied along the branch and extended his arm to clasp my hand. He lifted the toddler off my shoulder, then with one tug, he also pulled me out of the frigid water and onto the rocky bank. "Somebody get me a blanket," he shouted.

"Murph, help Trevor," I murmured.

"Somebody find Maverty. He's been down for too long," Murphy hollered as he passed the toddler to another paramedic and then scooped me into his immense arms.

"No. Save Trevor," I pleaded.

As Murphy carried me up the embankment, he glanced back in the direction of the accident scene. His expression made it seem like he was worried it was too late. I refused to believe that.

On the highway, Murphy laid me on a stretcher in the back of an ambulance. I couldn't move. I stared without blinking. The pounding of my heart in my ears slowed to a heavy, erratic thump. My body shuddered uncontrollably from the cold and the shock. Murphy wrapped me in a blanket and leaned on me, probably so his body heat would warm me faster. I screwed up the rescue. Murphy would have been able to focus on saving Trevor if I hadn't put the toddler in even more danger. Thoughts of Trevor not surviving because Murphy had to help me and the child crushed my chest. If he died, telling Kailyn it was my fault he drowned would destroy her. He had to survive. Not having him in my life would be unbearable. The shaking of my limbs turned into more of a seizure and Murphy got a panicked look on his face. He called out the back of the ambulance. I closed my eyes and wondered if it would be possible to will myself to die so I wouldn't have to live with the guilt of causing Trevor's death. What was I thinking? No. He couldn't die. No. No. No. I couldn't breathe.

# CHAPTER 8

In the emergency room, the nurses treated me for hypothermia with hot compresses and heated blankets. They wouldn't answer my questions about Trevor. Not knowing made me hysterical. "Please tell me," I begged. I tried to sit up, but one of the nurses held my shoulders to keep me down. Eventually, the other nurse opened the door and waved out into the hall. Two seconds later, Trevor entered the room, hair still wet. He rushed in and leaned over me to kiss my forehead. His breathing was heavy and the cold of the glacier water still pulsated off him, which sent goose bumps over my skin. He had a blanket wrapped around his shoulders and his chest was bare underneath.

"Oh my God. Are you okay?" I asked and squirmed to free my arms from the swaddled blanket so I could hug him.

"Yeah. I'm fine." He leaned back to study my face.

So relieved he was okay, I touched his cheek. It was so pale. "You scared me. I thought you drowned."

His eyebrows angled together and concern creased his forehead. "You scared me. I can't believe you did that."

"I was trying to save you."

"It was too dangerous."

"You risk your life for other people all the time."

"I'm trained." He slowly exhaled the stress he'd been holding in but it didn't seem to relax him that much. He shook his head as if he couldn't believe it turned out okay. "You could have been killed."

I held both his hands in mine and stared at his face. "I would rather die trying to save you than stand by and watch you die."

His expression tightened as if the thought of that caused him actual physical pain.

I leaned closer and whispered, "Watching you die would have been devastating. My entire world would have shattered and I don't ever want to feel that pain."

His eyes closed for a long blink and his fingers squeezed mine. It seemed like a million thoughts ran through his mind before he said, "It would have been devastating for me, too."

I flung my arms around his neck and hugged him so tightly it probably made it hard for him to breathe. He wrapped one arm around my waist and cradled the back of my neck to keep me close with his other hand. His muscles relaxed as I sunk into the embrace. Being near him had always given me a safe feeling. Being snuggled against his chest made me feel like everything in the universe was going to be all right, infinitely.

He ended the hug by kissing me on the forehead. Then he sat on the edge of the bed next to my hip. His mind was still racing, I could tell. But he didn't speak.

Eventually I asked, "How are the woman and the baby?"

"The woman has multiple broken bones. She's in surgery. The doctor thinks she's going to be fine. They helivaced the boy to Children's Hospital in Vancouver. He wasn't breathing when they put him into the ambulance. The paramedics got him going, though. Hopefully he'll recover."

"What is his name?"

"Joshua."

I nodded and did a silent prayer for Joshua. "The entire thing was so tragic and traumatizing. How can you do that all the time?"

"It's rewarding when they do survive." He smiled and squeezed my hand again. "You're an honorary member now. You saved two people with your vision. Four people, if you count us. I definitely would have driven right into the washout too if you weren't in the truck."

I couldn't help but smile a little because my visions were finally becoming helpful. In the past they hadn't been specific enough to save my dad or Giselle or the little girl Trevor and the Search and Rescue team tried to find in Iceland, but maybe this meant I could keep getting better at it if I practiced. "I'm glad it made a difference this time."

"I owe my life to you." He reached forward and ran his finger along my skin to lift the pendant Mason had given me. I had completely forgotten about it. "New necklace?"

I nodded and met his gaze.

"It's nice," he said as he let it slip through his fingers. "I didn't notice it before the party."

He obviously knew Mason gave it to me, and he didn't seem that thrilled about it. "It's from Paris," I said.

"Fancy."

I nodded, not sure what that meant. My core temperature rose, but it wasn't from the compresses. It was from the way Trevor looked at me. His expression was an intense mixture of terror and relief melted together. Seeing it made my heart race and my eyes water at the same time. "Will you lie with me to keep me warm?"

He nodded and moved to slide in next to me on the bed. We didn't talk about it, but the realization that we could have lost each other undeniably changed something between us. I knew he felt it too.

They kept us in overnight, which I wasn't thrilled about since Granddad would be sick with worry. And I was supposed to meet Paula to show her the breakfast routine. When Trevor and I walked out of the hospital together in the morning, the sky was clear and blue the way a July day was supposed to be. I was grateful for the sun. I'd seen enough rain and water to last me for a long time. The warm weather felt nice on my skin. The Search and Rescue t-shirt Trevor gave me to wear felt even better. It smelled like him and I hoped he wouldn't ask for it back. I turned towards the parking lot and he tugged my hand in the opposite direction.

"I thought we were going home," I said.

"We are, just not in the truck. The highway is still washed out, so I arranged for alternative transportation."

That was actually sort of good news because it meant Paula wouldn't have been able to get down from Squamish to Britannia Beach. I felt better for not standing her up, but Granddad was probably running around like crazy trying to handle the summer rush by himself. I let Trevor lead me down the sidewalk towards the marina. The Search and Rescue hovercraft was moored at the end of the dock. "Seriously? Isn't that a bit much?" I said.

"My dad has been itching for an excuse to fire it up. You don't want to disappoint him, do you?"

Not eager to make an even bigger deal about what happened, I said, "Maybe we could just catch a ride on someone's speed boat. All the guests from the Inn are going to be at the beach, rubbernecking at a hovercraft."

"Your grandpa will be there, too. I called him to tell him we're on our way." Trevor laughed at my embarrassment as his phone rang. He checked the call display, then glanced at me and excused himself as he walked away to answer it. I assumed it was his girlfriend Lindy because he spoke in whispers. I tried to decipher what he was talking about based on his body language. He had one hand in his pocket as he paced three steps in one direction, then turned and paced three steps in the other direction, repeatedly. His facial expression didn't change that much and it almost looked as if he was talking to a receptionist to make a dental appointment rather than to a girlfriend. Maybe that was what he was doing. He hung up and shot me a forced smile. "Sorry."

We walked down to the end of the dock and Trevor's dad Jim met us. He really did look excited to have a reason to use the hovercraft. "Hi, Deri. Are you feeling better?"

"Yeah. I'm definitely not cut out for the Search and Rescue profession, though."

"That's why we're here, but you do have a special skill set we all wish we had. If you ever want to join us we'd be happy to have you. Hop on." He held my hand to help me on board.

The hovercraft was the loudest and most ridiculous form of transportation. I cringed the entire way back to Britannia Beach, which only took a few minutes. We pulled up to the dock, and I was right, the beach was busy with guests from the Inn, along with other tourists who were hanging out because they couldn't get through to Squamish or Whistler on the highway. My granddad was waiting on the dock. I could tell he wouldn't be convinced I was all right until he could hold me in his arms.

I jumped out of the hovercraft and ran to give him a big hug. "Sorry if you were worried."

He leaned back to examine me. "I knew Trevor would keep you safe."

"Actually, she was the one who did the rescuing this time," Trevor said as he passed us.

I wasn't comfortable taking any credit since he did all the hard, life-threatening parts, but I was happy that my visions helped save the little boy. We walked across the beach and I focused on the sand to avoid the stares from the people. Trevor climbed the boulders that led up to the railroad tracks and turned to give my granddad a hand. He helped me up too, then we all crossed the highway.

The lobby of the Inn was completely filled with pink roses. At least ten vases, each filled with a dozen flowers. The fragrance was so strong it was almost intoxicating. I hadn't noticed at first that Kailyn was seated at the front desk, hidden behind the explosion of colour. She grinned as if she was in a magical dream world. "Read the card, Deri." Kailyn thrust her arm towards me. "Somebody loves Derian so much. Tell me what the card says. Tell me. Hurry. Maybe Riley Rivers will send me this many flowers before we get married. Read the card."

I glanced at Trevor, then opened the envelope and slid the card out.

*Dear Derian,*

*Although our first date did not go exactly as I hoped, I want you to know that I immensely enjoyed spending the evening with you. I would like to ask for a second chance at a first date. I hope you will do me the honour of accompanying me on a proper date this Saturday night.*

*Yours Truly,*
*M. Cartwright*
*PS I hope you enjoy the flowers, Miss Lafleur.*

"Who loves you, Derian?" Kailyn shouted impatiently.

My eyes met Trevor's and I folded the card into squares without answering her question.

"Chance Cartwright," Trevor mumbled as he walked out of the lobby.

My gaze alternated between Trevor, as he crossed the parking lot towards his house, and the note in my hand. The overwhelming smell of the roses made me dizzy.

# CHAPTER 9

Sophie had left me three phone messages. Each one was increasingly urgent as she hypothesized why I hadn't called her yet. She was down to two theories—either Mason had taken me on a private jet to a country where my phone didn't work, or I had been in an accident.

I plopped down on my bed and got comfortable because I knew she was going to go berserk when I called.

"Derian. What the hell? I heard the highway was washed out and I couldn't get a hold of you. I've been going mental down here."

"Sorry," I said calmly, just to bug her.

"Sorry. That's it?" Why haven't you been answering your phone? Is it good or bad news?"

"Both."

"Shut up, you guys," she yelled into the background. "You better start talking or I'll come home and beat it out of you," she threatened.

I explained the entire night and gave Sophie every specific detail from the McLaren, to Corrine saying I looked too pretty to be Derian Lafleur, to the flower necklace from Paris, and what Mason and I had talked about. I also retold with exact specifics of how Mason's face looked when Corrine kissed him and how Trevor's face looked when he was going to kick Mason's ass. When I told her that Trevor drove me home, she assumed it was the end of the story. I had to interrupt her to keep telling the rest.

I started with how I knew the highway was washed out and my vision about the kid. Sophie gasped at the other end of the phone when I told her the overpass fell on the car and I stupidly jumped in. I kept going without letting her ask questions and told her about getting washed downstream with the boy, spending the night in the hospital, the phone call from Lindy, the hovercraft, the room full of roses, and how Trevor got all moody and walked away.

"Holy shit. I'm on my way home," she said and hung up.

I was stunned she hung up on me, but I wasn't surprised she was coming home.

The entire band showed up in Britannia Beach after dinner. The guys were annoyed that Sophie made them come home early. Especially since the highway was still closed and they couldn't get up to Squamish. I told them I'd give them the key to my mom and dad's room if they promised to keep the noise down. I had to dust the room a little because it never got used—not that the guys would have cared if I hadn't. And it hit me that it was going to be Alan and Paula's room once they took over ownership. That was hard to accept, but I had no choice. I spent an extra minute to say my goodbyes to the space, the memories, and the past, then Sophie and I set up for an old-fashioned girly sleepover in my room with popcorn, nail polish, and waxing strips.

"Were you hurt at all when you were swept down the river?" she asked.

"No. My elbow is a little scraped. It was just really cold."

"Where's Trevor right now?"

I got up and peeked out my bedroom window. The light was on in his room. "In his bedroom."

She shot up off the bed and pressed up against the window. "That would be torture for me to know the man of my dreams was over there sleeping all alone in his bed only a stone's throw away from me. I wonder if he sleeps in the nude or maybe in boxer briefs. Ah, I'm making myself want to go over there to find out. How do you resist?" she asked as she flopped down on my bed.

"Thirteen years of practice."

"What did you think of Mason?"

I sat on my desk chair and clicked the top of a pen repeatedly. "He was nice to talk to. And he seems to be trying to figure out who he really is, which I admire. He's a really good listener and it feels like he's memorizing everything I say. He does this thing where he lets what I've said sink in for a while and then he says something super-thoughtful." I threw the pen on my desk because I was annoying myself with the clicking noise.

"All womanizers do that." She rolled onto her stomach and scrolled through photos on her phone. "They're trying to figure out your weak spots so they can take advantage of them."

"That's not what it felt like."

Sophie shrugged. "Maybe he's just really good at it."

I leaned over to share the popcorn with her, then sat back and balanced the bowl on my lap. "You make him sound so calculating. We have a connection that's real, I know that," I said with a mouthful of popcorn.

"I might be wrong about him. There's obviously something you find appealing about him. I know you wouldn't waste your time with someone who didn't have some genuine redeeming qualities."

"So, how did you and I end up friends?" I teased her.

"No idea," she joked back.

"This is going to sound stupid, but what I like about Mason are his flaws. There is something so vulnerable about him and he only lets me see flashes of it at a time."

"Well if flaws are what turn you on, there will be no shortage of guys for you to fall in love with." She tossed her phone down on the bedspread and stood up. She changed out of her clothes and put on one of my t-shirts to sleep in.

"I just like that Mason hasn't got it all figured out yet. Trevor has always been so together and steady. Sometimes he makes me feel like I need him for everything and he'll never need me for anything."

"Well, if Trevor is finally stepping up to the plate, this discussion about Mason is a waste of time," she hollered from the bathroom, where she turned the water on to wash her makeup off.

"If nothing happens with Trevor again, I would definitely consider a second date with Mason." I pulled my socks off to paint my toenails.

"You need to make it happen with Trevor, Deri. It's now or never."

No pressure.

Doug and the band were laughing way too loudly, so Sophie went next door to give them shit. I looked out my window again. The light went out in Trevor's room. It was only ten o'clock, so he must have been planning to get up early for a run. Or maybe the rescue took a lot out of him. He did seem uncharacteristically rattled by what happened. Apparently rescuing strangers was easier for him than watching people he cared about almost die.

I texted him: *How are you doing?*

*Good. Tired, though. How are you holding up?*

*I'm okay, but can we hang out tomorrow?*

There was a slight delay before he responded: *Yeah. I'll come over.*

When Sophie returned, I updated her as she straightened my hair for me. Then we both went to sleep with cucumber slices over our eyes.

# CHAPTER 10

When I got out of bed at five in the morning, Sophie mumbled something hostile and rolled over onto her cucumber slices. I dressed in dark jeans and a white tank top. My hair still looked good because Sophie had worked for two years in a beauty salon and knew how to make it stick straight. The door closed quietly behind me before I tiptoed to the kitchen to prepare breakfast.

By eight, the dining room was almost full with guests and the kitchen was packed with the band and Kailyn. The guys cleaned my parents' room for me and then helped with the breakfast dishes. After nine, when all the guests had gone down to the beach, Sophie and the guys headed outside to sit on the side deck. Doug helped me put the dishes in the cupboard. "Hey, Deri, do you have some Tylenol 3s or something like that?"

"Do you have a headache?"

He shoulder-checked to look out the window at everyone on the deck. "Don't tell Sophie, but my back is still killing me."

"From when you fell off the stage?"

"Yeah. I have to take something for the pain or I can't even stand up straight."

I frowned with concern at how he was standing, favouring his back. "That happened like three months ago."

"I know. It's not getting any better and the doctor won't prescribe me any more pain meds because it's been so long."

I glanced out the window and lowered my voice. "Why don't you want Sophie to know?"

He looked out at her again. "We have twelve shows booked in the next month. If she knows my back's still hurting, she'll bug me to cancel them. I don't want to let the guys down."

"Have you seen a chiropractor or something?"

"I will. I've just been too busy."

"Doug, you have to make time to do it." I stacked the last mug on the shelf and folded the dishtowel. "Wait here. I think my granddad has some pain medicine left over from when he had his surgery." I left Doug in the kitchen and went to get the prescription bottle out of Granddad's medicine cabinet in his room.

Kailyn was in the library pulling a puzzle box off the shelf when I walked by. The guy from 208 who lied about his credit card when he checked in was sitting in a chair by the window typing on his phone, so I called her and she met me in the lobby. "Do you mind doing the puzzle in the kitchen today?"

"Why?"

I nodded over her shoulder towards the guest. She turned and looked to see what I was getting at. "Do you remember what I told you?"

"Don't talk to him because he is a bad man."

"Shh." I gestured with my hands to make her lower her voice. "I don't want him to hear us say that, but I would be more comfortable if you did the puzzle in the kitchen today. Okay?"

She shrugged as if she didn't care one way or the other. She led the way back to the kitchen. Doug was waiting for me and he didn't look well. He was pale and sweating. I handed him the bottle. "You're probably not supposed to take these without a prescription."

He read the label and smiled. "It's fine. These are the same type the doctor has been giving me up until recently."

I soaked a towel in cold water to wipe his forehead. He shook a pill into his palm, then placed it on the metal pastry table and crushed it with a spoon. I watched as he brushed up the residue and swallowed it with a gulp of orange juice. "Why do you crush it?"

"It works faster that way." He shook the pill bottle. There were only three left. "Do you think your grandpa will miss the rest of these?"

"No. You can have them, but you have to promise to see a chiropractor or acupuncturist or something."

"I promise." He draped his arm over my shoulder and we joined everyone outside.

"Why didn't Trevor come over for breakfast?" Sophie asked as I sat down beside her.

"He sometimes doesn't come over when he knows it's busy."

"You're lying." Sophie pointed at me accusingly.

I rolled my eyes. "I don't know why he—" I paused mid-sentence because Trevor's motorcycle started up and he backed it out of their detached garage. He revved the engine and pulled forward to the edge of the deck with an extra helmet hanging from the bend in his elbow. "—didn't come over," I finished my sentence.

I glanced sideways at Sophie. She smiled and raised her eyebrow. Trevor flipped his visor up and motioned with his index finger for me to join him. I climbed over the railing and jumped down onto the parking lot. My heart beat so fast it felt as if I just climbed the mountain and ran back down.

"You want to go for a ride?" he asked over the sound of the engine. "I already talked to your grandpa. He said you should take the day off to recover."

I glanced over my shoulder back at Sophie. She scooted forward and sat on the edge of the chair as if she was about to watch her favourite part in a movie. "Sophie and the guys are waiting for the highway to reopen. I shouldn't just take off on them."

"The highway's open now. They built a one-lane temporary wooden bridge that will be in place while they rebuild. Murphy and his brother are coming down this way to go off-roading and drop my truck off for me."

The guys got up and all said, pretty much in unison, "We're out of here. Thanks, Deri." Sophie got up too and skipped behind the motorbike. She made a thumbs-up accompanied by a raunchy facial expression and a hip grind that only I could see, unless Trevor saw her reflection in the window.

"Have fun," she hollered as she got in the van.

"I was thinking you might need some therapy," Trevor said. He must have noticed my confused expression because he took his helmet off to explain. "You were already a little uneasy driving on the highway after your dad's accident. I don't want the washout to turn you into your mom. You should get right back in the saddle. Face your fear."

He handed me a leather jacket. It fit me perfectly, but was probably bought for Lindy. I smelled the collar to see if I could detect perfume. It just smelled like new leather. I couldn't summon visions at will, but I thought I would try to force myself to have a vision about whether I was going to die in a motorcycle wreck. Being all phobic like my mom was not appealing at all, so I concentrated on seeing my fate. My efforts didn't produce a vision. Instead, I was reminded of the guest in the library. "Is your dad going to be home?" I asked.

"Yeah, he's off today. Why?"

I hovered my lips right up next to his ear so he would hear me whisper over the sound of the engine. "There's a shady guest I don't trust with Kailyn. I told her to stay away from him, but someone should keep an eye on her just in case."

"Why do you have a bad feeling about him?"

"Shifty eyes. Lied to my face. Stared at her like a weirdo."

"Okay. Hold on." Trevor cut the engine and got off the bike, then jogged over to his front porch.

I watched as he took the stairs two at a time and disappeared into their house. It was going to be so strange to not live next door to him anymore. One of the reasons I thought moving to Toronto would be good was so I wouldn't have any visual reminders of the way things used to be. But I couldn't imagine a life without him in it, at least on the periphery somewhere.

Trevor stepped back out onto the porch and closed the door behind him before walking back to where I was waiting. "My dad's taking her fishing in a few minutes. It will be fine today. How long is he staying?"

"Until Wednesday."

"We should try to find out more about him when we get back." He handed me the helmet and said, "Your hair looks nice. Too bad the helmet's going to mess it up."

"Thanks." I tucked it behind my ears and stared at the ground to hide the flush in my cheeks the compliment had triggered.

We both put our helmets on and he slid his hands into leather gloves. I stared at the bike, not sure I could do it. Trevor sensed my trepidation and flipped his visor up. "Do you trust me?"

I nodded.

"With your life?"

Our eyes locked and his expression penetrated into my soul. Without a doubt I knew he would never let anything bad happen to me if he could help it. And he was the only person on the planet who made me feel safe enough to overcome my biggest fears. I absolutely trusted him with my life. "Yes."

"Then get on."

I swung my leg over to straddle the bike, then slid down on the seat until our bodies were touching. He shifted his upper body forward towards the handlebars, which pushed our hips even tighter together. That was new. It definitely felt like flirting. More than flirting, actually. It felt sexy. Everything inside my body warmed as I placed my hands on either side of his waist and leaned my chest against his back.

He yelled over his shoulder, "Move when I do, like we're one person."

The engine revved again, which sent vibrations through my already pulsating body and then we were moving. We rode slowly across the parking lot and turned onto the highway, heading south towards Vancouver. He changed gears and the bike thrust forward, faster and faster.

When we approached the curve in the highway where my dad's accident had happened, my heartbeat suspended motionless for one beat before it clunked back to life and then thumped out of control. The guardrail had been replaced and the skid marks had faded a long time ago, but the trees still showed the scars of where the car had torn through their flesh on its way over the cliff. The trauma still lingered in the shadows cast by the mountain and it coated me in dread every time I passed the spot.

Trevor reached his hand back and touched my thigh to check if I was okay. I wasn't really, so I rested my hand over his and gave it a little squeeze. I closed my eyes, took a deep breath, and whispered a list of reassuring self-talk, "I can do this. I don't want to be paralyzed by fears. Life is meant for living. When it's my time to go it's my time. I can't control destiny. Trevor would never let anything bad happen to me. Everything is going to be fine. Breathe."

We left the evidence of the carnage behind us and reached a straight stretch of highway. Trevor placed my hand safely back around his waist. Before I knew it, we were going so fast everything around us seemed to blur. When I realized he'd been holding back until that point, I shrieked and dug my fingers into the leather of his jacket. It was terrifying, so I repeatedly recited, "I can do this. I can do this. I can do this."

# CHAPTER 11

Thirty minutes after we left Britannia, we crossed the Lion's Gate Bridge and headed through Stanley Park into downtown Vancouver. Once we were off the highway, I felt a little more comfortable, but I couldn't think about the fact that there was absolutely no protection if another vehicle hit us. Travelling by car was going to feel perfectly safe compared to the bike since it, at least, had a giant metal cage protecting me. Scaring me was probably Trevor's plan all along. And it was the right thing to do.

I focused on the scenery instead of the thought of how much it would hurt if we had to dump the bike and slide across the pavement at fifty kilometres an hour. The English Bay area was busy with both foot and car traffic, so we slowed and inched bumper to bumper down Denman Street, people watching. After we crossed the Burrard Street Bridge, Trevor turned a couple of times and took us through the Kitsilano and Jericho Beach neighbourhoods and then up through an area called Point Grey. The houses were beautiful, with huge manicured yards. Eventually, we passed a large stone sign carved with the words: *The University of British Columbia.*

I had been to the campus a couple of times with Sophie to check it out, and we had come down to watch a football game in the fall. It was a beautiful campus that overlooked the ocean. U of T seemed nice too, from the pictures online, but Toronto itself wasn't as beautiful of a city. And it was bitterly cold there in the winter. And I didn't know even one other person going there.

UBC was the size of a small city with academic buildings, residences, private condos, stores, museums, theatres, and restaurants spread over the entire campus. Because it was summer session, the students who were wandering around and lounging on the grassy areas all seemed pretty relaxed. The vibe was inviting. As we drove past the row of the fraternity and sorority houses, I realized I needed to use the restroom. I slid my hand under the waistband of his leather jacket and gave him a gentle pinch, then flipped my visor up and yelled, "I have to pee."

He nodded and turned left at the next street. He parked in front of the Student Union Building and cut the engine. I got off the bike and removed my helmet. Once we weren't moving anymore and the engine wasn't rumbling, the rush caught up with me. My words spilled out way too fast and loud, and I was jigging around because the fear-induced adrenaline was still highly dosed through my bloodstream, and I really did need to use the washroom. "I can't believe I agreed to do that." I flipped my hair forward, shook it, and then ran my fingers through it to try to get the tangles out. I whipped it back and kept rambling, "I was petrified the entire time, but that's partly what made it so exhilarating." I thrust the helmet at him to hold and then I walked backwards for a few bouncy steps and said, "If I were you I would ride the bike all the time."

Trevor chuckled at my hyper rant and said, "The first time's always the best."

"Unlike sex." I said but then instantly wished I hadn't.

His eyebrows rose.

"Uh, not that I would know. Personally. I mean. I've heard. From other people." Desperate to shut myself up, I spun around and jogged into the Student Union Building.

So embarrassing.

After I finished in the washroom, I stood out in the concourse for a long time. The idea of getting back on the bike was awkward since he was going to know what I was thinking every time we accelerated, turned a corner, or came to a stop, for that matter. Walking home crossed my mind as a consideration. Eventually, I convinced myself that he wouldn't have read as much into the sex comment as I assumed he did. It wasn't like he could see into my thoughts, it only felt like he could. I decided that if I just pretended it meant nothing, then he would believe it meant nothing. But maybe I didn't want him to believe it was nothing. It was something.

There was a newsstand in the hall that had a magazine with Riley Rivers on the cover. A mini vision flashed through my mind. It wasn't like my other visions. It was more like a photograph. It was Kailyn's smiling face. I saw it for an instant and then it was gone again. My intuition was definitely on overdrive. The adrenaline didn't help. I searched my pockets and found a ten-dollar bill. The magazine was about Riley Rivers' North American tour and it was filled with photos, trivia, and information about the upcoming tour dates. She was going to go crazy over it.

Back outside, I tried to act normal, but Trevor looked superhot straddled on the bike. I couldn't stay cool. He smiled at me in a way that made it clear he was still amused by my sex comment. I handed him the magazine without saying anything. He tucked it into a storage compartment. "Is there anywhere in particular you want to go?" he asked.

Anywhere. Literally. I wanted to go wherever he wanted to go. Forever. But despite all the possibilities of things we could spend the day doing, I drew a blank. I needed to stall so he wouldn't decide to head home right away. "Since we're down here, maybe we should try to meet up with my mom for lunch. You know how she gets if she finds out I was in the city and didn't try to see her."

"Sounds good."

Definitely not the most romantic idea I could have come up with, but it would at least guarantee another couple of hours with him. And Mom really did hate it when I was in Vancouver and dodged her. I pulled out my phone to call her. She was working, but she was excited we were in Vancouver and insisted on making us lunch, so she invited us over to the condo. I talked to her for a little while, then hung up. "She said she can meet us in an hour at her place. Don't tell her about my involvement in the highway washout. She'll have a conniption."

Trevor nodded to agree because he knew her as well as I did. "The little boy survived. He's doing well."

"Really? That's a relief."

His eyes scanned down to my feet and then back up to my face, which was something I'd never noticed him do before. Then he smiled and said, "We make a good team."

"Definitely." I smiled too but hid it by turning to braid my hair. "What do you want to do for the next hour?"

"How about some more sightseeing around town? Get you used to the bike."

"Okay." Still grinning, I got back on and put my helmet on. When my hips slid down and pressed up against his, he subtly moved closer to me. There was definitely something going on between us. My stomach got butterflies and a zingy sensation shot along all my nerves. As we backed out and took off again, I closed my eyes and hoped he either couldn't read my mind or had the same thoughts going on in his head.

We rode back into downtown Vancouver over the Granville Street Bridge and toured around the city. The fear I had felt about being on the bike was completely cancelled by the comfort of being saddled up against his back. Taking a huge risk and feeling protected at the same time was invigorating. We rode through Chinatown, Gastown, and Yaletown, then he parked on the street in front of my mom's condo.

She lived on a tree-lined but urban street—completely opposite to Britannia Beach. There were always people around, jogging, walking their dogs, playing guitar, or whatever. She liked the buzz all night, but it was overwhelming to me with all the lights and the constant drone of the city grind in the background. The building itself was a modern high-rise with a doorman, nice if city living had been my thing.

I got off the bike. Trevor also swung his leg over the seat and hung his helmet on the handlebar, then he took my helmet and hooked it on the back of the seat. He raised one eyebrow in a sexy way and in one smooth move stepped towards me to place his hands on my shoulders. I studied his expression, trying to figure out what he was doing. The momentum of his body weight made me step backwards across the sidewalk until I was pressed up against the marble wall of the building. Oh my God, was he doing what it felt like he was doing? He leaned his body firmly against mine and slid his hands along either side of my neck. He was doing it. Completely taken off guard, I gasped when he clutched handfuls of my hair. Holy cow. It was happening. He paused and stared directly into my eyes, maybe to make sure I was okay with what he was doing. I was totally okay with it, so I pulled his face towards me and kissed him hard. He kissed me back with an intensity that reached every part of my body. The warm tingly sensation started in my lips, traveled down my throat, and into my stomach, where it transformed into a pulsating sensation that throbbed deep inside me and made me forget about everything but him. My heart pounded and my breathing sputtered as his lips moved with mine and his hands slid from my neck down my body. It felt as if I was in a dream. His right hand paused on my hip before he pulled me even tighter up against him. The blood rushed out of my legs and left them feeling as if they couldn't support my weight. My fingers dug into his shoulders to hold myself up.

I made the kiss as good as I knew how because I wasn't sure

if it was a one-time thing. It was actually better than good. It was mind-blowing. When he eventually stopped kissing me, he kept his face close to mine. His breathing was heavy and ragged, and his expression seemed torn, as if he was trying to decide whether he should continue or stop. He stared at me, maybe waiting for me to say something, but I was speechless.

It took a long time before I was finally able to construct a thought that was suitable for saying out loud. "You're really good at that," I said breathlessly.

The right corner of his mouth shot up in a grin. All of the tension drained out of his face and his expression became almost cocky. He knew he was a good kisser. I felt dizzy, so I unzipped my jacket to try to help myself breathe better. I sort of stumbled towards the bike and sat sideways on it. Passing out was a genuine concern based on how fast my head was spinning. With both legs stretched out onto the sidewalk, I propped my hands against my knees and inhaled as much air as I could manage. Trevor looked fairly pleased with himself as he watched my reaction.

Formulating what I wanted to ask him was not going that smoothly. Things like, *What was that? Does that mean you don't have a girlfriend?* and *Can we do that again, please?* were the questions that came to mind first. I exhaled slowly and studied his expression. "Why did you do that?"

"You didn't want me to?"

I blinked repeatedly to clear my brain. "I did. I do." I stood up. "I definitely wanted to kiss you. I just need to know what it means to you. I'm supposed to move to Toronto. Was it just a kiss to see what it might feel like or was it more than that?"

His cocky expression faded. "It was more than that."

I turned and paced on the sidewalk. I was so confused by all the conflicting emotions. What if it was only a reaction to the danger of the rescue and the fear of losing me? What if he was only saying it because he didn't like the idea of me being with Mason? Maybe he was as panicked as I was about the idea of not being a part of each other's everyday life anymore after the summer was over. Or was this it? Is that why he took me to tour around UBC? I spun around and faced him. "You want me to stay?"

His mouth moved as if he was about to answer but he stopped himself.

"Trevor. This is too important to not talk about. You need to tell me how you feel."

He rubbed the back of his neck and glanced down at his boots as he prepared what he wanted to say. After battling with some sort of internal conflict that was visible in his expression he looked up and said, "I want you to stay."

My mouth dropped open from the shock of hearing him actually say it out loud. My heart raced at all the possibilities. If I stayed, we could date seriously. We could maybe even move in together if things went well.

He stepped closer and held both my hands in his. "But you're right. This is really important. You've got a lot of big life decisions to make. Choosing what school you want to go to and where you want to live have to be based on what's best for you. I don't want my feelings for you to influence your choices. If you stay just for me and it doesn't work out you'll resent me. And I wouldn't be able to live with the guilt of knowing I held you back."

I nodded and let it all sink in. It was overwhelming to know that the option was there if I wanted to take it.

"Hellooooo," my mom's voice sang from behind me. I turned to see her coming up the sidewalk with a bag of groceries. "You're early. Sorry to keep you waiting." She kissed my cheek, then gave Trevor a hug. "Everything okay?" she glanced between us as if she could sense the emotional intensity.

"Yup," Trevor said as he took the grocery bag from her.

She pointed her finger into his chest and warned him, "You better make sure she gets back in one piece on that bike of yours."

"Will do," he promised. We all walked towards the front

entrance of the building together and the doorman stepped out to hold the door open. My mind was still swirling as we stepped onto the elevator.

"This is such a nice surprise." She hugged me again and then tucked my hair behind my ears. "You should come down to visit more often. I've missed seeing your face."

Her comment sounded sweet, but it struck a nerve and my bitterness made me tense. If she missed me so much, she could have made an effort to come up to Britannia Beach more often. Not wanting to drive on the highway was only her excuse for not visiting. There was a train. She could also take a boat if she was really interested. But she wasn't interested. The truth was she had hated growing up in Britannia Beach and if it weren't for my dad working in Squamish, she would have forced us all to move down to Vancouver when he was still alive.

She talked for the entire ride up in the elevator so didn't notice my animosity. Trevor did, though. He tilted his head to the side in a give-her-a-break type expression. He always had a soft spot for my mom because she had been there for him more than his own mom ever was. That wasn't saying much, but he was right. My mom wasn't horrible. And if my dad were alive he'd definitely be unhappy with me for making such a big deal of all the small annoyances. I shot him a less-than-enthusiastic I'll-try expression, which made him smile.

The elevator doors opened and my mom got out first. Trevor's hand slid across my waist to encourage me to go ahead of him. Wow. Every time he touched me it felt increasingly intense. The possibilities of what might happen next made me insanely excited.

After we entered the condo, Mom went on about something to do with the sale of the Inn and what Granddad was going to do afterwards. Trevor's hand slipped away from my waist and he bent over to untie his boots. I felt like I'd had one of those dreams you can't quite remember after you wake up. It was as if the kiss had happened, but it seemed too surreal to have actually happened. It occurred to me that it might have been one of my visions, which I was actually okay with, because if it was a vision it meant I was going to do it for real in the near future. I eventually decided it must have actually happened since I was still trembling. There was no way a vision could have made me feel the way Trevor did.

"Sweetheart, your cheeks are flushed, you're shaking, and you look as stunned as a bird that flew into the window. Are you okay?"

I nodded and attempted to act normal. Trevor grinned.

Mom made a delicious Thai lunch that she had learned how to make at a cooking class she was taking on Thursday nights. I tried not to stare too much at Trevor, but couldn't stop obsessing over the kiss and what it meant for the future. My stomach was too fluttery to finish my meal, so I got up and cleared the plates. Trevor and my mom chatted while I hid in the kitchen to recover from whatever the hell was going on. Sophie would know how to proceed. I slipped down the hall to my room to call her, but she didn't answer. She never did answer right away if she was busy rehearsing or waitressing. Or if she was just tired of dealing with people. I texted to let her know it was important, then sat on my bed.

The last time I had stayed in my room was at Christmas. It looked exactly the same. I hadn't redecorated it since I was about twelve, so it was kind of juvenile. The walls were painted a girly purple colour and the bedspread was a bold graphic floral that I had thought was cool when I was twelve. The only thing that felt current was the framed picture of Trevor and me standing on the dock in the winter time. Kailyn had taken the shot with her phone. It was my favourite picture because he was hugging me from behind to keep me warm.

Across the hall, I opened the bathroom medicine cabinet to see if my toothbrush was still there. It was, along with some shaving cream, aftershave, and a hair product for men. Items that obviously belonged to a man who wasn't my father. My hands shook a little as I squeezed toothpaste on my toothbrush and ran the water. I looked at myself in the mirror, hoping my expression would maybe give me a clue as to how I felt about the revelation that my mom had a boyfriend. Apparently, she was ready to move on. Three years was a long time to be alone. I just wasn't sure if I was ready for her to move on. It was weird to think of her with someone else.

I couldn't worry about that. My brain was already on full tilt trying to process things with Trevor. I spat in the sink and rinsed the toothbrush off before storing it back in the medicine cabinet. When I passed my parents' bedroom, I paused and peeked in the open door. Everything was new—the paint on the wall, hardwood floors, fancy bedding, and different artwork. It looked really nice. I scanned the bedside table and dresser to see if there was a picture of the new guy. There wasn't one, so I felt a little better.

Mom and Trevor had moved out onto the deck that overlooked the mountains. It was a view I had always loved because it felt as if we were looking towards Britannia Beach. As I squeezed between Trevor's chair and the railing, he touched my fingers. My eyes connected with his, then darted to check my mom's reaction. She wasn't paying attention, so I squeezed his hand before I sat down across from them. His smile was so sexy.

I wasn't sure if it was the date with Mason or the near-death experience that had finally shifted something in him, but I really liked it. My face was stuck in a huge grin and I felt dizzy at the thought of getting to kiss him again. The make-out session replayed in my mind repeatedly, but my mom kept asking me questions that forced me to concentrate. Eventually, I stopped daydreaming about Trevor and focused on her with more attention. I'd missed it before. The signs were all there. She looked fit, like she'd been working out; her hair was cut and styled kind of funky; she was wearing new shoes. She totally had a new boyfriend. I was choked that she hadn't told me, but in fairness, I probably wouldn't have reacted very well.

The visit was cut short because my mom's office called to track her down. She had to go back to work, so she walked us to the curb, hugged me tightly, and whispered, "I love you," in my ear. She gave Trevor another stern warning about his precious cargo before we got on the bike.

We waved at her and I hoped she would walk away and give Trevor and me the opportunity to talk alone. She didn't. She stood on the sidewalk to send us off. Trevor started the engine and we pulled away from the curb. I didn't want to look back in case it threw the bike off balance and made us crash right in front of her. She likely watched us ride away until she couldn't see us anymore. Trevor reached his hand back and touched my thigh again to see if I was okay. I squeezed his hand and then hugged him as tightly as I could. Although it wasn't an official date, it was the best date I had ever been on. I couldn't wait to get home to pick up where we left off.

We pulled up by the front door of the Inn and parked. I got off the bike and we both took our helmets off. I stood near the handlebars, studying his expression, which seemed really happy.

He smiled and asked, "Did you have fun?"

"Yes." I was almost giddy. "Do you want to come in and—"

"Trevor!" Kailyn shouted and stormed across the parking lot. "Lindy Jacobsen is mad at you. She came here to see you and you weren't here. Where have you been?"

Trevor appeared as shocked as I felt when a tall, fit, blonde woman stepped out of the house onto his porch. She leaned against the post with her arms crossed. He whipped his head back to me. My heart dropped to the pavement with a painful thud. He definitely would have seen the sting in my eyes before I turned and rushed into the Inn.

# CHAPTER 12

Through my bedroom window, I watched Trevor walk towards his porch. Lindy stepped forward and wrapped her arms around his neck to hug him. He hugged her back with one arm, then turned and looked at my window—he knew I would be watching. I pulled the curtains shut, threw the helmet on my bed, took the leather jacket off, and chucked it to the floor. Then I texted Sophie: *Crisis. Come over, ASAP!*

While I waited for Sophie to either call or show up, I took a shower to try to calm down. I was mad that Lindy was literally next door. But I really had no right to be. Why did he make a move if she was still in the picture? Things were already complicated enough without adding cheating into the mix. That made everything so much harder. Or, maybe not. Maybe it was easier. It was just a kiss. It must not have meant as much to him as it did to me. It felt like it did, though. Or, maybe she showed up at his house for some other reason. He wasn't the type to cheat on someone. There might be a simple explanation. Likely I was overreacting. I didn't even know what was going on. I needed to talk to him before I jumped to any conclusions—and died of a shattered heart. Communication. Clarification. Don't assume the worst until the worst is confirmed.

Feeling slightly better, that there might be hope, I got out of the shower. With one towel wrapped around my body and a second one around my hair, I checked my phone to see if Sophie had called back. She hadn't.

A knock at my door startled me. Unless Sophie had already been in her car and on her way to Britannia Beach when I sent her the text, it wasn't possible that she could have arrived so quickly. My stomach tensed and my heart raced when I realized it might be Trevor. I wanted to talk to him, but I was also scared too. What if the worst was about to be confirmed? Or what if it wasn't? Ugh. I didn't know what to do.

"Deri," Kailyn shouted through the door.

Equally relieved that it wasn't Trevor coming over to tell me everything that happened was a mistake, and disappointed that it wasn't him coming over to say there was a simple explanation for Lindy being there, I put a robe on and let her in. "Hey, what's up? Come on in."

"Thanks for the Riley Rivers magazine. I love you. Trevor said you bought it for me. Did you like your date with Trevor?"

"Did Trevor call it a date?"

"I don't remember." She sat down on my desk chair.

"Do you know what Lindy is doing at your house?"

"She's Trevor's girlfriend."

"Are you sure?"

She didn't answer because she was distracted by her magazine. She flipped through the pages and kissed the pictures she liked the most. I decided it would be better for my sanity if I didn't try to pump her for information. I needed to talk to Trevor directly to put myself out of my misery, one way or the other. Hopefully Lindy wouldn't stay too long.

Kailyn closed the magazine and looked right in my eyes. "Do you love Trevor as much as I love Riley?"

"Yes," I moaned and crossed the room to curl up on my bed with my face buried in the pillow.

"Do you want to marry him?"

"Yes," I mumbled from behind the pillow.

"Do you want to make babies with him?"

"Yes."

She giggled and got up to leave. She left the door wide open, so I had to drag myself off the bed to close it. Sophie called before I got back under the covers. The entire story spewed out of my mouth like emotional vomit. With the phone wedged between my ear and shoulder, I walked over to the window and moved the curtain with the back of my hand to peek out.

"You guys kissed!" Sophie shouted into the phone.

"Mm hmm."

"How was it?"

"Unfreakingbelievable."

"And Lindy was standing on the porch just waiting for him?"

"Mm hmm."

"What's she like?"

"Stunning—drop-dead gorgeous. I should have stopped the kiss, not that I wanted to. If my boyfriend kissed another girl like that, I would be choked."

"Trevor isn't the type of guy who'd cheat. I'm positive he would have ended it with her before pursuing anything with you."

"Not if he hadn't planned to pursue anything with me. He was definitely surprised to see her, but they hugged like a couple. Maybe it's all just a big misunderstanding. I need moral support while I wait for her to leave. Can you come over?"

"I'm on my way." She hung up.

When I noticed the red Honda Civic parked out front of his house, I got back into bed and stared at the ceiling.

Sophie showed up half an hour later with two dress bags in each hand. She rushed into the room and hung the bags from the top of my closet door before lunging towards the window and sticking her face through the crack in the curtain. "Is that her car?"

"I guess." I pouted.

"Don't worry. He's going to be so sorry when he sees what you look like when you go on your date with Mason."

"I can't go on a date with Mason. I'm a total wreck."

"You have to go on a date with Mason because you're a total wreck." She unzipped the dress bags and pulled each one out. "These are my mom's. She has so many she won't even notice they're gone. Here, try them on." She held up a clingy blue dress that draped over one shoulder.

"I don't feel like trying on dresses. I didn't even accept Mason's invitation."

"You'll feel better when you see how hot you look. I promise."

I shook my head. "You were all Team Trevor the other day and now you're rooting for Team Mason. Make up your mind."

"I'm Team Derian. Boys come and go. All I care about is that you're happy. And that you're pushing yourself out of your comfort zone once in a while."

I pointed at her. "And you like the drama."

"Yeah, that too."

"I rode on a motorcycle. That was out of my comfort zone."

"And it felt amazing, right?"

"Yes," I admitted and flopped back against my pillows.

"What team do you want to be on?"

"Trevor's, but I can't believe he would do that to her, or me. The thought of him being with her hurts so bad," I moaned and clutched chunks of my hair.

"So hurt him back with Mason."

"I don't want to hurt him back, and I don't want to use Mason."

"Going out with Mason will force Trevor to make his decision." She tossed the black dress towards the bed and it draped over my waist. "Jealousy is the best motivator for guys."

"I don't want to use Mason to get Trevor to dump his girlfriend and ask me out. It's mean to everyone. And honestly, if I have to resort to manipulation tactics, it obviously isn't meant to be."

"I am almost one hundred percent positive Trevor is not dating Lindy. Once she leaves you can talk to him like a big girl and ask him what the deal is. Until then, just try a damn dress on."

"Fine." Because I knew she wouldn't stop harassing me until I tried at least one of them on I got up and picked a red one that was tight at the waist and tailored to angle sharply in at the knees. It was sleeveless and had a conservative neckline at the front, but it was cut in a sexy V down the back. It had a skinny belt that matched and I liked it because it looked like something Audrey Hepburn would have worn in the old movies that my granddad watched.

Sophie showed me how to do my hair in a sophisticated up-do. Then I looked in my closet for the heels I borrowed from her. I couldn't find them and remembered why. "Shit. I left them in Trevor's truck," I said.

"I'll go bust the window."

"He doesn't lock the doors."

"Too bad. I feel like misbehaving." She flexed her skinny bicep and curled her lip to make a tough face.

"Haven't you done enough misbehaving for a while?" I stood sideways in front of the mirror and checked out the profile of the dress.

"If you're referring to that skank I dropped at the bar, she deserved what she got."

I turned so she could undo the zipper. "Yeah, yeah. She tried to touch Doug's business when he was on stage. I know."

"She didn't try. She actually grabbed and squeezed him like he was a damn cow that needed to be milked. It's not okay to molest another girl's guy. Besides, I saw her the other day and she looks a million times better with her new nose. I did her a huge favour."

I shook my head as I took the dress off and pulled on a pair of sweat pants. "You're a menace."

"You know it. I'll be right back." She left my room and came back less than a minute later without the shoes. "His truck's gone and so is his dad's. Lindy's car is still there, though."

I looked out the window. "They must have gone on a call. I wonder why she stayed."

Sophie's expression made it seem like she didn't think it was a good sign, but she didn't say anything.

As I stared through the glass, I had a vision: Trevor spun around and locked eyes with me. His face was haggard and tense. He was working, looking for something. Someone. Kailyn.

When my eyesight came back into focus, Sophie stared at me, waiting for details of what I saw.

I sat on my desk chair and massaged my temples. "My visions have been out of control since I got back. I could really do without them since my mind is already ridiculously cluttered with other problems."

"What did you see?"

"Trevor was trying to find Kailyn. His face looked beat up." I frowned as the scenes from my vision combined with my concerns about the guest in 208. "I'm worried it has something to do with a guest who checked in the other day."

"Like he's going to abduct Kailyn?" she asked as she pulled out boxes from my closet.

"No. I don't know. It could be nothing." Or maybe it was something. My last few visions had been more accurate and useful. Maybe it was better to take it seriously, even though it didn't feel dangerous. She seemed happy when I saw her face. But maybe that was because she didn't know she was in danger. "Do you think Doug could do some hacking and find out more about the guy just from his name?"

"If he's using his real name."

"Good point. Psychopaths probably don't usually go by their birth names." I sighed and brainstormed ways to find out more about the guy without actually looking like a lunatic myself.

Sophie rummaged through my closet. "Don't you have any nice shoes?"

"That cream-coloured box has a pair of silver strappy heels that I wore when I was in my cousin's wedding party."

"Ah yes." She held them up as if she had found the Holy Grail. "These are perfect. Was that the wedding where you had to wear the purple stripper dress?"

"Uck." I rolled my eyes. "Don't remind me."

"There are probably still a bunch of guys who have that picture as their screensaver."

"Fantastic," I mumbled.

# CHAPTER 13

The next morning, I set up for breakfast. Trevor and his dad's trucks were both back. Lindy's car was still there, too. Vomit brewed in my stomach when I realized she had obviously spent the night with him. A simple misunderstanding that could have been cleared up in a quick conversation suddenly felt like a giant knife to the back that was going to be a little more difficult to explain. I quickly got everything ready for the buffet, then woke Granddad to tell him I wasn't feeling well. He got up and took over.

Literally sick, I curled up on my bed and stared at the wall. It was such an asshole move for Trevor to ask her to spend the night right after we kissed and he told me he wanted me to stay in Vancouver. It was very uncharacteristic. He could be aggravating with his moods and the way he withdrew sometimes, but he had never been an asshole before. I could accept that I couldn't compete with his super-model college girlfriend, but he didn't have to mess with my emotions and rub my face in it. It was cruel. And not the way he would normally treat anybody, let alone me. There had to be an explanation. Unless I had imagined the entire interaction in Vancouver. Or maybe it did happen and he regretted telling me how he felt and wanted to take it back. Did it hit him afterwards that it felt weird to kiss someone he had been friends with almost his whole life? Was he trying to be a jerk on purpose so he wouldn't be a factor in my decision to stay or go? Apparently he didn't realize it did influence me, pushing me in the leaving direction. Nothing made sense. I was too confused and sick to even cry.

At ten, Granddad knocked on my door and came in. "How are you feeling, sweetheart?" He placed a tray with toast and juice on the table for me.

"Not great. Sorry to leave you stranded on your own."

"You did almost everything, and have you forgotten that I managed just fine all by myself while you were in Europe? I'm not retired yet."

"That was before the busiest part of the season."

"I'm fine. And Alan is here now to work the front desk." He sat on the edge of my mattress and checked my forehead for a temperature. "Trevor was asking for you. He wanted to come down to see you, but I told him you weren't feeling well. Was that the right thing to do?"

"Yeah. I don't want to talk to him right now. Was a blonde girl with him?"

"Yes. She seemed like a nice young lady."

My face grimaced, so I tried to hide it.

He patted my shoulder. "Get some more rest. Being in that cold water might have taken more out of you than you thought. Alan and I can handle things out front."

Ironically being swept down the river in a near-death experience had been easier to deal with than facing the truth that Trevor was out of reach. When Granddad stood to leave I asked, "Did the man from room 208 bring his driver's licence down for you to copy?"

"He didn't give it to me but Paula might have done it yesterday. I'll check. Why?"

"I got a weird vibe from him. Maybe monitor him and don't let him talk to Kailyn."

He nodded and his eyebrows angled together in concern because he knew my instincts were a little stronger than the average person's gut feeling. "He's out right now, but I did see him asking Kailyn about something she was drawing. I'll keep an eye on him when he gets back."

"Thank you."

After he left, I decided to go over and talk to Trevor. Partly because if I didn't it would bother me all day. And partly because I knew there had to be more to the story about why Lindy slept over—other than them having sex. It didn't make sense to sit around making myself sick over hypotheticals when all I had to do was walk up and ask him.

I grabbed the helmet and the leather jacket and stepped out the emergency exit into the parking lot. Jim's truck was gone but Trevor's 4Runner and the red Honda were still parked out front. I headed to their front porch, but stopped when I noticed Lindy sitting on the rocking chair. She was so beautiful. Her skin was flawless and she didn't even appear to have any makeup on.

"Hi," she said. Completely pleasant. "I'm Lindy."

"Hi. Nice to meet you. I'm Derian."

"Yeah. Trevor has mentioned you before."

I nodded, wishing I had waited until she was gone. "Is he around? I need to talk to him."

"No. He and Jim got called out to another rescue just after breakfast."

"Another one. Wow. They've been unusually busy lately." Like ridiculously out-of-the-ordinary busy. I stepped up on the porch and placed the helmet and jacket on the bench. "I borrowed your things because Trevor needed to give me a ride into Vancouver yesterday. I hope you don't mind."

She glanced at the helmet and jacket, then smiled. "I don't mind at all. You can borrow those anytime."

I retreated back to the steps and glanced around the village to give myself time to think whether it would be better to come up with an exit strategy or a way to pump her for information. "Trevor wouldn't have offered to give me a ride and lent me your things if he had known you were coming."

"That's my fault. I was away visiting my parents in Comox and came home early as a surprise. He didn't know." She leaned back and crossed her legs to get comfortable. "I thought since we might be moving in together in the fall it would be a good idea if I met Jim and Kailyn. And you, of course. He thinks of you as a sister, too."

Meeting the family because they were going to be living together was not the explanation I was hoping for, or even remotely prepared for. The shock of it nearly dropped me to my knees. I reached for the railing to steady myself and smiled to fake some composure before I said, "Getting a place together is a big step. How long have you two been together?"

Her expression made it seem like she was pretty impressed with herself. It bordered on smug. "We met in September and were really close friends at first. Things got serious gradually. He hasn't talked about our relationship with you?"

"No. He's kind of private when it comes to girlfriends."

"How about you? Are you seeing anyone?"

"Um." I swallowed hard, trying not to wince from the excruciating pain of suffering through the conversation with her. "No. Nothing serious." I pointed over my shoulder. "I should probably get back to the Inn. Are you staying long?"

"Just until they get back. Trevor asked me to watch Kailyn because you have some sort of dodgy guy staying at your Inn or something."

Her tone was almost accusatory but she was good at covering the bite with a sweet smile. Maybe I was just bitter, but her fakeness bugged me. "If you need to get going I'd be happy to keep an eye on her. I usually do. The rescues can take hours, sometimes they even go well into the night."

She smiled, but it wasn't pleasant. It was a warning. "I can stay as long as they need me to."

Message received. "Great. Well, nice meeting you." I turned and walked away, wishing I could shrivel up and disappear. Her stare felt like a laser in my back. Obviously she knew something happened between Trevor and me. Or if she didn't know for sure, she was smart enough to realize it was a concern.

Trevor was not the person I thought he was, and that actually hurt more than anything else. His integrity used to be one of things I admired most about him.

After I ducked into the lobby my phone buzzed with a text from Mason: *No pressure, but I wanted to make sure you got my note inviting you out tonight. If you're interested, let me know. No worries if you aren't. I'll understand.*

The summer was supposed to be fun, right? Going on a date with Mason would be fun. Not serious. Not long-term. Not emotionally consuming. A relationship between Trevor and me couldn't be temporary and casual. Even if Lindy wasn't in the picture, committing to something with Trevor would have meant staying in Vancouver, living with my mom, and throwing away a scholarship. And there were no guarantees it would have worked out. It was better to not put myself through the drama only to end up where I started again, completely crushed. Mason was the easier choice, or at least he was the easiest way to distract myself while my first choice was busy sleeping with his first choice. In an impulsive reflex that might have been entirely fueled by wanting to show Trevor I had options, I replied to Mason: *I'm interested. What time should I be ready?*

*Six. I'm looking forward to it.*

*Me too. See you then.*

The only thing that would keep me from completely obsessing about Trevor and Lindy was to stay busy. I placed orders, wrote cheques for our suppliers, restocked the pamphlet display, watered all of the plants, washed the windows, folded towels, and even helped the maid service with some of the rooms.

While I was in room 208, I took a look around to see if I could find out anything about the guest's true identity. Besides the no suitcase thing, there was nothing out of the ordinary that I could see. The only remotely revealing clue was a poker chip from the casino. It was on the table with his pocket change. I felt guilty for snooping, so I let the maids finish without me.

I had no name to go on and he was out in his car, so I couldn't even ask Doug to check the plate. At least Kailyn was safe when he wasn't around. If that was even what the visions were trying to tell me. I was so messed up, it was impossible to know.

At four-thirty, I was sitting at the front desk with my granddad when Trevor and his dad finally got back from the rescue. They'd been gone since before nine, so it must have been a pretty big rescue. To avoid seeing Trevor and Lindy together, I made up the excuse that I had to get ready for my date and rushed to hide in my room before they could see me.

It was the longest amount of time I had ever spent getting ready for anything. After a long bath, I moisturized my skin with a cream that had a sheen to it and made my skin look silky smooth. I rolled my hair up and clipped it the way Sophie had showed me. Then I shimmied myself into the dress. Sophie's mom was stick thin, so her dress fit my curvier body tight in all the right places. I put on the necklace Mason had given me and slid my feet into the silver strappy heels. When I saw my reflection in the mirror I couldn't help smiling.

My phone buzzed with a text message. It was from Trevor: *We need to talk. Please.*

I looked out the window. The red Honda was gone. I texted him back: *I have nothing to say to you.*

I threw my phone down on my bed and took deep breaths so I wouldn't ruin my makeup. It might have been possible to forget that he had a girlfriend if Lindy had never showed up. With her perfect face seared on the back of my eyelids, it was impossible. Seconds later, there was a knock on my door. "Deri, open the door."

I didn't know what to do. He obviously knew I was home and I couldn't exactly jump out the window in my outfit. My stomach twisted into a knot and I started to sweat. I flailed around for a few seconds, trying to come up with some way to avoid him. Unfortunately, I was going to have to face him at some point anyway. The most mature thing was to just get it over with. I swung the door open almost violently.

His body jolted back as if he was stunned or something.

"I thought you wanted to talk. Speak," I said coldly. My lower lip trembled a little, so I bit it to make it stop.

"You look amazing."

"Save it," I said and tried to slam the door back on him.

He braced his arm and blocked the door. "Derian, please let me explain. May I come in?"

"No. I'm on my way out."

"Please just let me come in and—"

"I'm not interested," I interrupted.

He stepped sideways and filled the doorway. "You're the one who is always asking me to talk about things. I'm here. I want to talk about what happened."

"Oh really? You want to talk about the fact that you made out with me and told me you don't want me to move to Toronto, then came home to find Lindy—who was supposed to be away visiting her parents in Comox—standing on your porch?"

He frowned, wondering how I knew that. "You talked to her? What else did she say to you?"

"It doesn't matter what she said. It matters what you did. Did you really think I wouldn't notice that she spent the night? Then to add insult to injury, you brought her here for breakfast in the morning. That was really mean." I grabbed my phone off my bed and stuffed it into my purse. I squeezed past him to get out of my room. "There is literally nothing you could say that would make this all right." I stormed down the hall towards the lobby and hoped that Mason had already arrived to pick me up.

Trevor followed me out into the parking lot. "At least give me a chance."

"Okay. Do you have a good explanation for why you would ask me to stay in Vancouver when you already had plans to move in with her in the fall?" My back was to the water and I heard the noise before I saw what made it. A helicopter landed on the dock.

Trevor's expression creased, completely confused. "Lindy told you we were moving in together?"

"Yes, she did. Among other things."

"It's not true."

"No? Well, then she's as unclear about the status of your relationship with her as I am. Maybe you need to sort that out." Mason got out of the helicopter and hopped down from the dock onto the sand. I looked over my shoulder and said, "Evidently my date is here. I have to go."

Trevor scoffed as I walked away from him. "A helicopter might be a first even for Chance Cartwright."

I turned back towards him. "Why do they call him Chance?"

Trevor laughed scornfully. "He wouldn't tell you, would he?"

"He wanted me to form my own opinion of him."

"Chance is short for 'No Chance'. They call him that because when he goes after a girl she has no chance to resist him. They say he's never met a girl he didn't score with."

"Well, if he at least has the decency to break up with the current girl before he pursues the next one, he has more integrity than some guys. Right?"

Trevor frowned, then glanced across the highway at the helicopter. Something shifted in his expression, as if he surrendered. Not like he had no defence. More like he wasn't willing to fight. Frustrated, I turned away from him and rushed to meet Mason.

When I eventually looked back over my shoulder, Trevor was gone.

# CHAPTER 14

Mason met me at the edge of the highway, smiling. He looked classy in a tailored charcoal-coloured suit with a white shirt, a shiny black tie, and what looked like really expensive dress shoes that were getting dusty from the sand.

"You look exquisite," he spoke closely into my ear so I could hear over the sound of the helicopter.

I smiled and mouthed, *Thank you.*

He kissed my cheek and then scooped me up to carry me across the beach. I held on tightly around his neck and turned my face towards his chest because the helicopter blades were spinning and the wind whipped sand at us. When we reached the dock, he put me down and held my hand to escort me into the helicopter. He shut the door and we were in the air before I even had enough time to consider the potential danger. Definitely outside my comfort zone. Sophie would have been proud.

My life felt crazy, like I was spiralling out of control in a whirlwind of bizarre events. The party, the highway washout, kissing Trevor in Vancouver, and then literally lifting off the beach with a millionaire playboy in a helicopter. It was surreal. I took a deep breath and exhaled slowly to try to ground myself in reality. It didn't really work. I still felt like I was in a dream, which was enforced by the fact that the view from the helicopter was mind-blowingly spectacular. Although I'd lived in Britannia Beach my entire life, I had never seen it from that perspective—like a painting with azure skies, sapphire mountaintops, emerald old-growth rain forest, and turquoise-and-jade water. The helicopter banked from side to side as we followed the coastline towards Vancouver.

Mason touched my knee and pointed out the window on his side. I leaned over to see what he was showing me. It was a pod of Orca whales breaching below us. It was so cool. Mason smiled with the whitest and straightest teeth I had ever seen. He reminded me of the Ken doll I used to make my Barbie kiss when I was little.

The helicopter banked again and we flew over the towering trees towards the North Shore. In what seemed like an impossibly short amount of time, the city appeared in the distance. We skimmed over the buildings and then hovered above one of the high-rises downtown. The pilot lowered the helicopter and landed on the roof of the building, then turned off the blades.

Mason climbed out first and helped me step out. "That was incredible." I beamed.

"Not a bad way to travel, I have to admit."

"Where are we?"

"My office. Do you want to see where I work?"

"Definitely."

Mason spoke with the pilot to tell him what time to pick us up and then tugged my hand to rush me into the building before the blades started whirling again. We took an elevator down just one level and it opened up into a lobby that looked like a five-star hotel. One of the walls was entirely covered in slate and water cascaded down it in a waterfall. The evening sun angled through a huge skylight in the roof and onto the receptionist's desk. No one was there and the lights were on half-power, so it was very quiet and sort of soothing, like being at the day spa.

94

"It's beautiful," I whispered. "You must love working here."

He shrugged. "I haven't actually spent much time in the office."

We walked down the hall past framed archive pictures of Vancouver, which were hung art-gallery style. He opened the double wood doors of a corner office, stood to the side, and made a sweeping motion with his arm to invite me in. Two floor-to-ceiling glass walls revealed a panoramic view of the ocean, city skyline, and the mountains. It put my mom's balcony vista to shame. The desk was teak with clean lines. The chairs were modern chrome art pieces. Whoever decorated the space had impeccable taste.

"Is this your dad's office?"

"No, it's mine." He sat down at the desk and put his feet up. "Doesn't it suit me?"

"Wow." I scanned the paintings on the wall and items on the book shelf. "You're a bit young for an office like this."

"The benefits of nepotism."

I sat in one of the chrome chairs, just so I could run my palms over the gorgeous lines. "The other employees must hate you."

He laughed. "They did when I first started." Then he winked and added, "I've used my charm to win them over."

"Ah yes." I stood and gazed out the windows. "The incomparable Chance Cartwright. Your reputation precedes you."

"Maverty told you, didn't he?"

I spun around to face him. "He might have said something about me having no chance."

"From where I'm sitting, I'd actually say your chances are very good."

"Oh, really?" I stepped closer, rested my hands flat on his desk, and leaned my weight forward on my arms. "You should probably know that I'm not a huge fan of helicopters, and I will be the one who decides whether you have a chance with me, not the other way around."

His eyebrow rose and he bit the corner of his lip for a second before he responded, "I can live with that. I am remarkably charming, though."

I smiled and shook my head to concede. "I'll give you that."

He stood and leaned in as if he was thinking about kissing me. I glanced at his lips, wondering what it might feel like if he did make a move. Then his weight shifted away and he grinned. "Are you ready for our next stop?"

Not sure if I misread his cue or if he was being a tease, I exhaled the breath I had been holding and nodded. "Lead the way."

We took the elevator to the ground floor and walked over to a black Lincoln Town Car that was waiting with a driver. The driver opened the door and called Mason Mr. Cartwright. He drove us to a museum I'd never been to before. Mason had obviously made arrangements for us to go in after hours. A security guard, who also called him Mr. Cartwright, let us in and turned on the lights. As soon as the gallery lit up I realized what it was and I gasped as my legs jiggled in excitement. "Mason. Oh my gosh. John Lautner is my absolute favourite?"

"I know."

I clapped, unable to contain my excitement. "How could you have possibly known that?"

"The better question is how could I have possibly gotten this collection out of California."

My gaze hopped around to absorb all the photographs, architectural sketches, and models. "What? Are you joking? You had the collection brought here just for us to view?"

He nodded and wrapped his fingers around mine to lead me towards the first glass case.

Wow. "Mason, this is incredibly thoughtful, but ridiculously extravagant. I wish you hadn't gone to the trouble or the expense just for me. It's overwhelming."

"All it took was one phone call. Someone owed me a favour. Don't even worry about it."

"This is unbelievable. You are unbelievable. Thank you."

He smiled in a modest way and said, "I'm glad you like it."

I more than liked it. It was one of the highlights of my entire life. I was mesmerized and could have spent days studying the sketches and 3-D models. Mason tried to be as interested as I was and he asked lots of questions, but I could tell they just looked like a bunch of funny-shaped buildings to him. "I'm sorry. This is boring to you."

"No, not at all. I could watch you smile like that all night."

He knew all the right things to say. All the right things to do. Who did things like bring the collection of a person's favourite architect to town for a private viewing? I glanced at him repeatedly, hoping to catch a clue to prove he was too good to be true. All he showed was the genuine enjoyment a person gets from doing something they know makes others happy. Maybe in his case, just because it was too good to be true, didn't mean it wasn't true. Trevor saying *no chance* echoed in my head and made me cautious, though.

When I finished looking at the entire collection, I turned to Mason, still dumbfounded. "Seriously. How did you know?"

"It's a secret. Are you ready for the next stop?"

I exhaled and considered the question. "I'm not sure. You kind of blew me away with this stop."

"Good."

If he was only trying to reel me in for one reason, I was in trouble. The Lautner exhibit firmly imbedded the hook in the corner of my mouth. It was very easy to go with the flow and find out what other surprises he had planned for the night, and it was possible, that at some point, I'd have to rip the barbed point from my flesh and flail to change course. But so far, it didn't seem necessary.

Mason thanked the security guard and we got back in the Town Car. The driver took us to Caffé dé Medici. My face likely shifted into an expression of incredulous shock when I saw the awning above the door. My dad used to take me to Caffé dé Medici every year on my birthday. There was only one other person in the world who knew that. "Did you talk to my mom?"

Mason lifted his eyebrows in an amusing way but didn't answer. He just grinned and helped me step out of the car. He rested his hand lightly on my waist to guide me into the restaurant. The maitre d' called him Mr. Cartwright and seated us at a private reserved table in a quiet corner of the restaurant. It was staggering to imagine how much work he had to put into researching and planning the date. I couldn't quite decide if it was romantic or over the top—either way, it was impressive. Was I supposed to research him before we went out? I didn't even think to check whether he had social media accounts. He could be wanted on a worldwide warrant, for all I knew.

After the waitress poured lemon water in our glasses, I asked, "What other intimate details do you know about me?"

"Test me."

"When is my birthday?"

"Too easy—August thirtieth."

"Middle name?"

"Marie, after your maternal great grandmother."

"What did my dad do for a living?"

"He was an environmental engineer and he worked mostly in the forestry industry."

"You must be good at your job. But it's easy to find information that's likely available online. What baked good is my specialty at the Inn?"

"Hmm. That one is a bit of a trick question since I have never been invited to join you for breakfast. I did hear Maverty going on about your apple cinnamon muffins once, so I'm going to go out on a limb and say that they're your specialty."

I shook my head in disbelief. I was captivated, not so much by the amount of information he had collected, but by the fact he'd even bothered. Womanizers didn't put that kind of effort into just trying to score. Did they? Maybe an obsessive stalker would work that hard to study the object of their affection. In Mason's case I really felt like he was genuinely interested and just happened to have the research tools at his fingertips because of what he did for a living. If he was trying to intrigue me, it was working.

He had on a silver watch with a black face that had several dials on it for different time zones, different than the one he had on the night of the party. "What was I wearing on our first date?" I asked, to test if his observation skills were as good as his research talents.

"Seriously?" He chuckled. "You underestimate my abilities. Just so you know, I consider this our first date. Taking you to the party was an error in judgment on my part. And I can actually tell you what you were wearing the very first time I ever saw you."

"Really? That was a long time ago."

"It was my first day at school after I moved to Squamish. You were in the eleventh grade and you were wearing a beige mini skirt with brown-suede boots and a light-pink sweater. The night of the party you were wearing sexy jeans and a purple top."

"Holy shit, you're good. I remember your first day at school too. Sophie and I were watching you and gossiped about how hot you were."

"You thought I was hot?" He grinned.

"You were all right," I teased.

"I thought you were more than all right."

I could feel my face go red. "Okay smarty pants, if you know so much about me, what kind of car have I always dreamed of owning?"

"A McLaren." He laughed. "Just kidding. I don't know that one."

"A 1963 Corvette Stingray. Nobody knows that, so I guess I cheated."

The waitress took our orders and brought a basket of warm

bread. Mason wrapped his hand around my wrist and turned it to expose my elbow, which was scabbed. "How did you do that?"

"Oh, that's just a scratch from the highway washout the other night."

His expression locked into something stuck between disbelief and intrigue, as if he couldn't tell if I was joking or telling the truth. He thought about it a bit longer and then looked concerned. "That was you? I heard the story that two motorists saved the woman and child. I didn't realize it was you. What happened?"

I told him the story and he listened attentively. Memorizing his expressions was like trying to learn a new language. Every nuance was interesting and challenging at the same time. I finished with the part about the roses in the lobby and said, "And now you know everything about me. I feel bad I don't know as much about you."

"That's what dates are for. You're just going to have to agree to a series of dates in order to make up for the deficit."

I shook my head and shoved his shoulder lightly. "I don't have enough nice dresses for a series of dates with you."

He raised his eyebrows and grinned at something that he was obviously thinking about. I could only guess what was going through his mind, probably the thought of something crazy like flying a New York designer to custom fit me for a new wardrobe. Wondering what type of surprises he was capable of was exciting and overwhelming at the same time. His world was obviously drastically different than the one I was used to, and I didn't know if that was a good thing or a bad thing.

"Seriously, though," I said. "I'm just a simple girl. This is all nice, but I'm used to very basic things. You don't need to go all out."

"Dinner at your favourite restaurant is a fairly standard gesture."

"I guess, if you don't include the mode of transportation, chauffeur, and private art show."

He chuckled. "If you think this is overboard, good thing I didn't fly you to New York."

"You considered it, didn't you?"

He laughed and nodded.

God, he was so cute.

Our conversation was really engaging and easy as we ate dinner. I learned that when he was about to say something funny, his left eyebrow twitched. When he was uncomfortable, he licked his bottom lip before he talked. When he was impressed by something I said, he smiled my favourite shy smile. I resolved to say more impressive things.

"Okay, I have another question." I sat up straight in my chair and rested my elbows on the table. "If you liked me for so long, why didn't you ask me out before you went away?"

"You were dating Steve." He finished the last of his vegetables and slid the plate to the side of the table as the busboy refilled our drinks. "What ever happened to that guy?"

"He and his family moved to Calgary in October. I still email him every once in a while to see how he's doing. He applied for Harvard. I'm not sure if he got in or not."

"You're definitely a nicer person than I would have been in that situation." His mood deepened into something more serious as his gaze danced across the features of my face. "Do you want to know why I really never forgot the impression you left on me?"

I nodded, curious.

"Even though you smiled and hung out with your friends like nothing was wrong I knew exactly how heartbroken you felt inside. Even before I heard what happened to your dad, I could see it behind your eyes. And I understood it because I felt the same way."

"Really?" I sorted back through my memories of that time. "You lost someone you loved, too?"

He nodded and ran his finger over the nick in his eyebrow. "My brother. Cody. He died of cancer."

"I'm so sorry." I reached over and covered his hand with mine. "Cody Cartwright. Is that what the CC on your tattoo represents?"

He nodded and seemed curious as to how I knew about his tattoo.

"When we were at the Britannia pools last summer I noticed it. The date was the same year my dad died, so I wondered about it back then."

He reached for his glass of water and took a sip. "Sorry to dampen the mood. It's not the most cheerful thing to have in common."

"Don't apologize. It feels nice to know someone who appreciates how devastating a loss like that is. Everyone around me was always very sympathetic and patient with me as I grieved, but they could never fully comprehend the hole it left, no matter how much they wanted to. It might sound crazy, but I'm glad we share that."

He smiled and leaned in to kiss my cheek. "Me too." The waitress came by. Mason told her we would be passing on dessert and he slipped her his credit card. He must have seen the disappointment in my face because he said, "Don't worry, there will still be dessert. Later."

I smiled and rested my hand on his. "Even though everything is way fancier than I'm accustomed to, I'm having a nice time. The best time, actually."

"That's good." His fingers squeezed mine. "I was nervous since you flat out told me I wasn't that impressive to you."

"I'm sorry I said that. It's the Chance Cartwright playboy thing that's not that impressive to me. Mason is impressing me, so far." I lifted my head to meet his gaze. "I like the stripped-down version of you."

"Literally?" He laughed and stood to pull my chair back for me.

"Ha ha. Although the literal interpretation would probably still stand, I meant it figuratively. And, just so you know, I like you in the suit. It's classy. And sexy."

As we left the restaurant, he smiled in a way that made me melt inside. I was hooked and reeled, which was astonishing given that we were still in the getting-to-know-each-other phase. Charming was an understatement.

The Town Car driver drove us back to Mason's office, and the helicopter was already fired up when we walked out onto the roof. We flew back up the coast and right past Britannia Beach to Squamish and then lowered down towards the flat roof of a house that was located in a remote area on a cliff overlooking Squamish. The helicopter dropped us off and flew away back in the direction of Vancouver. Mason hadn't given the pilot any instructions about when to pick us back up.

Uh oh. Time to rip the hook out. It was a great date, but I wasn't spending the night. I looked around and scrambled to come up with a way to get myself home. I should have said something while we were still in the air.

He sensed my apprehension and said, "Don't worry. I'll drive you home later."

Later. Yeah. Later after what? "Um, I'm sorry, Mason, if I gave you the wrong impression, but I'm not the kind of girl who sleeps with a guy so soon." Or at all, for that matter. "I had a fantastic time but I should probably go home now. Sorry."

He chuckled. "That's not why we're here. I want you to meet my parents."

"Oh." I clenched my eyes shut, feeling awkward for assuming. "Okay," I choked out past my embarrassment.

He seemed amused by my humiliation and wrapped his arm around my shoulders as he led me to the door. We went into the house and a woman rushed up the stairs to greet us. She was tall and had long limbs. She wore tight jeans that most women her age wouldn't have been able to pull off. She was almost bouncing on the spot as she waited for Mason to introduce us. "Mom, this is Derian Lafleur. Derian, this is my mom, Juliette."

"It is so nice to meet you, Derian," Mrs. Cartwright shook

my hand with both of her hands. "Mason has never brought a girlfriend home to meet us before. You must be very special to him."

My face got hot. When I looked at Mason, he smiled his shy smile. "My mom insisted on making chocolate fondue for dessert."

"Yum."

We followed her down the staircase past a gallery of family pictures. I walked slowly to view each of the images. Then I stopped and stared at one that caught my attention. "You were twins?" I asked him.

Mason's expression creased, but he forced a smile as he nodded. Mrs. Cartwright turned and climbed back up the steps to stand near us.

"I'm so sorry for your loss," I said to her as I leaned in to get a better look at the next picture. It was a photo of both boys holding up fish that they had obviously caught. "You guys look so happy in that one."

"That was at our grandparents' cabin in the Okanagan."

Mrs. Cartwright smiled as she remembered. She ran her finger along the picture frame and said, "When Cody got really sick, we wanted to make his last wishes come true. We asked him if there was anything in the world that he wanted to do. We thought he would want to see the Pyramids, swim with dolphins, or go on an African safari. But instead, he chose to visit his grandparents at the cabin so he could go fishing one last time."

Mason licked his lower lip. I slid my hand into his and held it tightly. The obvious change from having two identical boys in every photo to having just one made my heart ache. He stretched his arm around my shoulder and pulled me in as we walked down the stairs to the kitchen.

Mason's dad joined us for chocolate fondue. He wore what he likely considered casual clothes—white-linen drawstring pants, white-leather square-toed loafers, and a long-sleeved, light-weight, white sweater. He looked as if he stepped out of a Calvin

Klein photo shoot. His hair was salt-and-pepper coloured and cut nicely. He was the thin kind of fit, like Mason, not quite as tall, but he had a powerful presence. "Nice to meet you, Derian," Mr. Cartwright said as he shook my hand firmly. "Mason has told us a lot about you."

"It's nice to meet you, Mr. Cartwright. You have a beautiful home."

"Thank you. Mason says you plan to study architecture. Do you have any idea who designed the house?"

I looked around at the squared horizontal wood beams, the skylights, the glass walls, and concrete flooring. "Is it an Arthur Erickson design?"

He nodded, impressed that I got it right on the first try. "You should come back in the day so I can show you the exterior. Other people think it's ugly. Hopefully you'll appreciate it."

Mason's mom was standing behind his dad. She smiled and mouthed silently, *it's ugly.*

Mason laughed.

"I'm sure I would appreciate it," I said, trying not to smile at their teasing.

"There you go, Mason, I just locked in another date for you." His dad chuckled as he dipped a segment of banana into the pot of chocolate. We all hung out at the kitchen island huddled around the fondue pot. Mason's dad did the same eyebrow thing as Mason when he was about to say something funny. I got a sugar high from the chocolate and ended up laughing so hard at all of his dad's stories from his most recent trip to Abu Dhabi. My favourite had to do with a camel, an outhouse, and an episode of streaking. Mason didn't laugh and I wasn't sure if it was because he had heard all the stories before or if he was just uncomfortable hanging out with his parents.

Maybe sensing Mason's mood, his dad eventually said, "Come on, Juliette, let's leave these two alone and have a little date night of our own." He leaned over and tickled her waist.

His mom squealed, said good night, piled the dishes in the sink, and ran up the stairs with his dad chasing behind her.

Mason squished his face. "Sorry about that."

"They're cute," I reassured him.

Mason washed the dishes, then took my hand and showed me to the home theatre room. The room was dark, with no windows and there were several leather couches and recliners arranged in front of a screen. A shelf full of trophies and medals for basketball, rugby, and hockey hung on the back wall.

"Wow. You're a good athlete."

"Not anymore. I blew out my knee in grade twelve and ended my career."

"Oh right, I remember when you were on crutches."

He nodded and smiled at the memory. "That was the first time you ever really spoke to me. Do you remember that?"

"Yes." I leaned my butt on the back of one of the couches and crossed my arms as he stepped behind the wet bar.

"Would you like a glass of wine?" he asked.

"Oh, no thank you. You go ahead. I'll just have water."

He slid the bottle of wine back in the rack and grabbed two waters out of the fridge. Then he turned on the microwave to pop a bag of popcorn.

I smiled as I remembered back to that day in high school. "You don't know this but that day at school when you were on crutches I stood in the hall and waited until you got to your locker just so I could offer to help you. I convinced myself I should do it to be nice because I couldn't bear watching you struggle with the crutches and your books. But really, I just wanted the excuse to talk to you. I even rehearsed a couple of conversation starters in my head so you wouldn't think I was dull."

"Really?" He glanced at me. "I wasn't sure if you really knew who I was before that."

"Everyone knew who you were, Mason."

He shrugged as if it was news to him. "I would have asked you out then, but you were dating Steve."

He handed me the bowl of popcorn and I had a vision: Something broke, snapped. Then I fell for a long time. I landed on something hard and cold, smashing my cheek and ribs. It hurt to breathe.

"Derian." Mason squeezed my arms.

My eyesight came back into focus and he looked concerned. "Sorry."

"What happened? Do you have epilepsy or something? You kind of blanked out for a second."

"Interesting." I smiled to play it down, then moved to sit on the couch and ate a handful of popcorn. "The amazing Mr. Cartwright doesn't know everything about me."

"Should I take you to the hospital?"

"No. It's not epilepsy. Don't worry."

"What is it?"

My visions weren't something I felt comfortable sharing with most people. Unfortunately, it had been happening with unusual frequency that did border on some sort of mental-health problem, even by my standards. So, if we were going to hang out more, he'd eventually have to know about it. "If you make it to the next date I'll tell you everything," I promised.

I tugged on Mason's hand to force him to sit down on the couch beside me. He still looked concerned about my well-being, which was sweet. I pressed buttons on one of the remote controls to get the movie to play. Obviously, I pressed the wrong things because Mason smiled and took the remote away from me.

"So, what are we watching?" I asked.

"My sources may have failed to mention that you experience seizures. However, I was informed that you are a fan of eighties movies, especially John Hughes films."

I grinned as the opening scene of the movie started to play.

"You're not actually going to sit through *Pretty in Pink* just for me."

"Yes. I like how it ends. Plus, if you sit close enough to me I won't really be paying attention to the movie."

I took off my shoes and snuggled in next to him, completely relaxed. He wrapped his arm around me and I rested my head on his chest. The No Chance nickname crossed my mind. There was a possibility it was true, but not for the reasons I was worried about. Unlike the other guys I had dated—although my experience was limited and not a valid sample to compare to—he didn't use the movie as an opportunity to make out or get gropey. We just snuggled. It really didn't feel like his plan was to sleep with me and then dump me. Maybe I was naïve but it felt more like he actually wanted to spend as much time as possible with me. Admittedly, that kind of attention was intoxicating. If he did make a move I might be too lulled into a comfortable stupor to resist.

"Derian," he whispered as the credits rolled across the screen. "It's late. I should drive you home."

I groaned a little because I was too tired to get up. "I can sleep here on the couch."

"That won't help my reputation at all," he joked.

I sat up slowly and grabbed my shoes in my hand, but I was so sleepy. My upper body flopped down onto my lap. "I won't tell anyone I slept here."

"Maverty will know," he said and scooped me up. He carried me to the garage, then propped me up against the wall as he opened the passenger door of the McLaren.

I sank into the leather seat and rested my head back as he walked around to the driver's side. Once he got in, I said, "I had a really nice time. Good job."

He smiled at the compliment and started the engine.

"This was by far the best date of my life."

"I agree." He kissed my cheek softly before he backed out of the garage.

We were back in Britannia Beach in what seemed like minutes. It might have been because I was tired and relaxed, or maybe because Trevor's bike therapy had worked, but I didn't even care how fast Mason must have been driving. He pulled up in front of the Inn and ran around the back of the car to open the door for me. I stepped out and leaned up against the hood, expecting a goodnight kiss. He did his shy smile and inched closer. His hands slid up to rest on either side of my jaw and he gently pulled my face towards his. His lips lingered closely to mine to tease me. "Good night, Derian," he said and then pulled away.

Well played. Not kissing me was obviously a calculated move on his part. And I had to admit it worked. I studied the features of his face one more time and smiled. "Good night, Mason."

The 4Runner turned off the highway and the headlights lit us up for a second before it pulled into the parking lot and stopped in front of Trevor's house. We both watched Trevor hop out of his truck and slam the door. He stepped up onto the porch and disappeared into his house.

I looked back at Mason, who seemed interested, but unfazed by Trevor's timing. His arms were wrapped comfortably around my waist.

I glanced at Trevor's bedroom window, then at the porch where Lindy had stood waiting for him. A slight pang of guilt needled in my stomach for rubbing my date with Mason in Trevor's face. On the other hand, I was free to do whatever I wanted. His shitty timing was his fault, not mine. I stepped back from Mason's embrace and said, "Thank you for a very memorable evening."

"What are my chances for another date?"

"It's a definite possibility." I smiled at him over my shoulder as I walked away. He was still sitting against the hood of his car grinning when I closed the door and turned out the light.

# CHAPTER 15

At five in the morning, I was surprisingly alert and energetic given the limited sleep. I hurried to get everything set up for Sunday breakfast before the high of my date with Mason wore off and the sleep deprivation caught up with me. Trevor didn't come over at all. No surprise, but it felt weird to know he was just next door avoiding me. I was going to have to talk to him at some point because I couldn't stand having awkward feelings between us. The conversation would have to wait until I really missed him, though, otherwise my anger would make it go all wrong.

Paula wanted to work the front desk by herself for practice, so once the dishes were done, I went to my room to relax. My photo albums were already packed into boxes and prepared for my move, but I pulled out an older one and flopped onto my bed to flip through pictures of Trevor and me growing up. He had his red baseball hat on backwards in almost every shot. I smiled thinking about that hat. I used to steal it just to make him chase and tackle me. He would straddle his legs and sit on my chest until I said mercy. I tried not to say mercy for as long as I possibly could. Unfortunately, I couldn't breathe and eventually had to give in. His dad always got mad at him for fighting with me and made him stop because I was a girl, so I got smart and started stealing the hat only when his dad wasn't around.

Because my parents were keeners with the camera, there were a lot of photos. One that made me stop flipping the pages was a picture of Trevor and me standing next to a tranquilized black bear. It had wandered into the village and was rummaging through garbage bins. After conservation officers sedated it to relocate it, Trevor and I posed beside it pretending we captured it. My dad snapped the photo, then the bear moved and growled, which made me scream and run. Trevor didn't run. Instead, he jumped over the bear and stood between it and me. Thankfully, the bear flopped back down, still in a daze. Trevor was always crazy brave like that.

There were photos of us on the raft we had made with logs and a sheet from the Inn for the sail; in the tree fort we built for sleepovers; beside the totem pole we tried to carve with an axe; and outside the igloo we dug into a snow bank after a huge storm. The last picture in the album was a picture of my dad and me that Trevor had taken with our camera the winter before my dad died. We were snowshoeing and there was a family of deer on the trail behind us. The forest was silent that day and the fresh snow made everything perfectly still. We could hear the deer breathing. It was a cool shot.

All those memories of my dad and Trevor were going to fade away once Paula and Alan took over the Inn and I wasn't living in Britannia Beach anymore. I didn't want to think about it so I closed the album and closed my eyes to take a nap.

Just before noon, my phone rang with a call from my mom. "Hi baby. How are you doing today?"

"Okay, I guess." I got up and went into my bathroom to brush my teeth. "How are you?" I asked with toothpaste foaming in my mouth.

"I'm hanging in there. Are you planning to go to the cemetery?"

It took me a second to figure out what she meant. With all

the drama, I had totally forgotten it was my dad's birthday. "Uh, I haven't really made plans yet. I will probably go, though." I brushed my hair and put a little bit of makeup on to hide the fact that I had just woken up.

I left my room and headed to the library as my mom continued to talk. We discussed my dad and the sale of the Inn for a while, then she asked about Trevor. I was able to avoid telling her what happened and distract her with questions about U of T. She was excited about me going to her Alma Mater, and even though it had likely changed drastically in the last quarter century since she was a student, she filled me in on everything about it. I thought about asking her about her boyfriend but then decided it wasn't the best timing. Eventually, she moved on to a story about a woman at work who contracted some weird disease. I was only half listening because the guy from room 208 was pacing back and forth in front of the Inn. He was on his phone and appeared agitated. I threw in a few 'mm hmms' at the appropriate junctures in my mom's story. The guy hung up, looked around as if he thought he was going to get jumped, then pushed his glasses up on the bridge of his nose and unlocked his car. I headed into the lobby and wrote down his licence plate, then stared at him as he backed out of the parking spot. Before he turned the wheel to pull away, he paused and looked directly at me. I didn't care that he caught me staring at him. I wanted him to know he was being watched. I smiled at him the same way I would to any other guest. He didn't smile back. He just drove away.

Mom finished her story. Apparently, the woman found some miracle cure in Southeast Asia. "How are things going with that Cartwright boy?"

"What?"

"Mason. You've been dating him, haven't you?"

Paula was at the reception desk, so I ducked into the empty dining room and sat at a table by the window. "Um, not really. He took me on one date. What do you already know?"

"He called me at work and introduced himself. He told me where he works and where he lives and he asked me what some of your favourite things are. He seems nice and I know his family is well off."

"What difference does that make?"

"Well, with someone like Mason you would have more opportunity to travel and meet influential people. I know you adore Trevor, but face it, he's a Search and Rescue junkie like his dad. He's not going anywhere. He'll always live under that bloody mountain risking his life for strangers, and one day he just might not make it home. And then what?"

"And then what?" I repeated, strangely furious. She had triggered an anger that I didn't even know was inside me and my mood took an instant and crazy one-eighty. My first instinct was to hang up on her. Instead, I raised my voice and started ranting, "And then what? Well, if I ended up with Trevor in the future and he didn't make it home one day, I'd send our daughter to live with you so she could take care of you as you get old." I stood and squeezed my eyes shut. "And then what? Well, then she'd raise herself and I'd just call her once a week or so to make sure she hadn't turned into some sort of delinquent." I was pretty much yelling into the phone. "And then what? Well, then without telling my daughter, I'd just go out and get a new guy and let him move into the home I used to share with Trevor. Then I'd pretend like my old life never happened and I'd forget about the one day that he didn't make it home. And then what?"

"Derian Marie!" What has gotten into you?"

I clenched my eyes shut, instantly regretting the tirade. I lowered my voice, worried that Paula probably heard. "I'm sorry. Things have been weird and stressful lately. I got hardly any sleep last night and I'm feeling really pressured about my future. And I'm upset that I forgot Dad's birthday. I don't know why I said those things. It was out of line. I'm so sorry."

Mom was silent on the other end for a while before she asked, "You know about Ron?"

"I didn't know his name. I saw some men's things in the medicine cabinet when I was over for lunch. I assumed it meant you were seeing someone."

"And you're not comfortable with that?"

I sat back down and used my thumb to apply pressure to the knot of tension forming in my neck. "I don't know. Everything is just coming at me too fast and all at the same time. I need some time to think and sort out how I feel."

"Okay." Her tone sounded more hurt than accepting, but a least she wasn't angry.

"I'm sorry I snapped at you. I'll call you when I'm feeling better."

"Okay. I love you."

"Love you, too." I hung up feeling like an awful person. It wasn't fair to dump my mood on her. And I was embarrassed that I still acted so immature around her. "Grow up, Deri," I mumbled to myself.

I turned the corner back into the lobby, braced for Paula's reaction. Fortunately, she had moved into the library and was busying herself by cleaning the windows. Whether it was lucky timing or if she had done it on purpose to avoid the awkwardness of over-hearing my hissy fit, I was relieved.

Trevor and his dad both ran to their trucks and took off for another Search and Rescue call. The same vision from the night before flashed through my mind again: Something snapped. I fell. My cheek hit something hard and all of my breath was knocked out of me. The pain was excruciating.

"Are you okay?" one of the guests asked as he stared at me.

Apparently not. "Yes. I'm sorry." I shook my head to focus. "May I help you with something?"

"Beach towels."

"Sure, here you go." I handed him four towels and recorded his room number. "Have a great day."

"Are you sure you're all right?" he asked again.

"Yes, I'm fine. I was just daydreaming. Sorry."

He didn't seem convinced. I wasn't either. I was pretty sure Trevor was going to get hurt on the rescue.

# CHAPTER 16

The guest who asked for the towels left for the beach with his family. I debated about whether I should warn Trevor about my vision or not. If I was wrong, I didn't want to distract him while he was on a rescue. But I couldn't pretend that my visions hadn't been getting stronger and more accurate. If I was right, I didn't want to live with the knowledge that I could have prevented him from getting hurt.

I finally decided to text him: *Be careful.*

After not getting a response I looked up from the phone to see Mason pull into the parking lot and park the Range Rover. He hopped out and walked towards the front door, wearing a white t-shirt, grey cargo shorts, and canvas slip-on shoes.

He stepped into the lobby and smiled. "Hi."

"Hi." I didn't know what else to say. I was honestly shocked to see him.

"Sorry to drop by unannounced." He ran his hand through his hair. "I don't want to seem like I'm coming on too strong, but I have a bunch of work projects over the next couple of days and I'm going to be really busy. I was worried if I waited too long to ask you out again you would assume I didn't have fun last night. And I did, so I was hoping to take you for a picnic lunch today. Nothing fancy. If you want to." He studied my expression, which was likely hard to read since I didn't know exactly how I felt. "Are you hungry? I already packed everything. It's in the truck."

A picnic did sound nice. I glanced at the clock. Trevor was going to be gone for a while. I wanted to go out to visit the cemetery anyway. Paula had things under control without me. Getting outside to enjoy the weather might be good for reducing my stress. And sorting my feelings. Plus, he already packed the picnic and drove down.

I nodded to accept the invitation. "Sure."

I told my granddad I was leaving and met Mason at his truck. He drove north on the highway, so I asked if we could make a quick stop. Then I pointed to signal him to take the turn off to the cemetery. The road wound around and once we passed through the gates, I directed him to stop the truck near where my dad was buried. "It's my dad's birthday. I just want to say hi. I'll only be a minute."

He nodded, completely understanding.

I hopped out and walked over to the headstone. It looked a little neglected, so I brushed away the dirt on the surface and ran my finger over the carving of his name. "Hi, Dad. I'm sorry I almost forgot your birthday. I'm totally scatter-brained right now. You wouldn't be very proud of me. I yelled at Mom today and it was baaad. She probably won't get over it for a while." The wind picked up and swirled my hair into my face as if he was listening. "Did you know she has a boyfriend? I hope you're okay with that. She's happy and I should probably be okay with it, but based on my flip-out today I'm not yet. I know you would want me to try harder to get along with her. It was going pretty well until I found out about the boyfriend." The air became very still and birds sang in a tree not far away. "Trevor and I kissed. Maybe you would rather not know about things like that, but I can't talk to Mom about it. Everything is messed up, though, because

Trevor's girlfriend Lindy showed up and slept over at his place. I was really hurt and to kind of get back at him I went on a really amazing date with someone Trevor doesn't like very much, which was probably a bad idea since I'm playing with people's feelings—mine included. Speaking of which, that's Mason in the truck over there. He's actually really nice, but I always believed Trevor and I were meant to be together. Now I'm confused. It seems like if it was meant to be it wouldn't be this hard. Right?"

My phone buzzed with Trevor's response to my earlier text: *Thought you had nothing to say to me.*

*I had a vision. Just be safe.*

*Always am. Can we please talk when I get back?*

I debated because living with the uncertainty of our future together seemed a thousand times more desirable than knowing for absolute sure that we could never work. Talking about it was the adult thing to do, though, so I texted back: *Yes.*

I sighed and closed my eyes, trying to hear my dad's advice or see his face. It didn't work and I didn't want to keep Mason waiting for too long, so after a few minutes I stood and kissed the headstone. "Mason's brother Cody is with you. Can you make sure he's not alone? Thanks for listening. Happy Birthday. I miss you and I love you."

Mason watched as I approached the truck, but as I got closer he looked away so it would seem as if he wasn't. I climbed into the passenger seat and closed the door. The radio was on a low volume.

"Thanks for waiting. Do you go to the cemetery to visit your brother on your birthday?"

"Sometimes. Cody's buried in Ottawa, though, so I don't get to go as much as I would like."

"I'm sorry."

He reached over and touched my cheek tenderly. His sensitivity made me smile. "Ready for lunch?"

I nodded.

We left the cemetery and drove along the highway to a wilderness area popular with locals. After parking the truck, we hiked the trail towards the top of the waterfall. Mason carried the picnic basket and I carried the blanket. Trevor and I had spent almost our entire childhood in the forest together—climbing trees, making forts, caving, rock climbing, and cliff jumping, so even though I was wearing flip flops, I climbed faster than Mason. Once I reached the top I spread the blanket on a grassy spot that wasn't under the cover of the tree canopy. The sun was warm and the sounds of birds, chipmunks, and running water were so peaceful.

"Geez, you're like a mountain goat," Mason said when he caught up to me.

"I had to learn how to be quick to keep up with—" I stopped myself before I said Trevor's name. "My legs are long."

He smiled briefly with only half his mouth as if he knew what I had meant to say, then he opened the picnic basket and set up the dishes.

"Thanks. This is nice," I said as I stretched out on the blanket to soak up the warmth of the sun.

"A simple, stripped-down date. Especially for you." He passed me a Perrier water.

"*Merci.*"

"Ah, that reminds me. We need to go back to Paris again sometime. Not just at the same time, but actually together."

I studied his expression. He was serious and it was absolutely not a big deal to him to say things like that. It was a strange feeling to imagine a relationship with him that might progress to something like travelling the world together. The type of nervousness I felt right before I took a risk to do something outside my comfort zone.

When I didn't respond, his smile faded and he said, "Sorry. I didn't mean to get ahead of myself. But I do want to make your dreams come true. And money is no object. Anything you want. Just say the word and I will make it happen."

"I guess people who have grown up with a lot of money take it for granted." I sat cross-legged and unwrapped one of the turkey paninis he had packed. "You don't need to do extravagant things to impress me."

"What impresses you?" He popped a green grape into his mouth and leaned back on his elbow.

"Honesty."

"That's it?"

"That's it."

He thought for a minute and then his eyebrow arched before he said, "Well, I honestly want to take you to Paris."

I laughed. "You're being provocative again." I reached into the picnic basket and offered him some cheese and crackers. "Why don't you just give people you? If they don't like it that's their loss. If they do, then you know for sure they are a real friend."

His head hung and he was quiet for a long time. "Maybe I don't know how to give people that."

"Why?"

He shrugged. "For more than half my life I was Mason and Cody. He was always on my left side and I was on his right side. We didn't do it consciously. He was just always there. Then that was gone. I was completely lost and had no idea who Mason was without Cody. As I got older, I tried to be the rich kid, Chance, Mr. Cartwright, or whoever people expected me to be because at least I knew who that was. You are the first person in a really long time who has asked me what Mason thinks or feels about anything. I don't know how to give you Mason because I'm not sure I know who I really am."

I nodded as I processed. I loved his honesty and his willingness to be vulnerable. I smiled and tossed a mandarin orange at him. "Well, based on the glimpses I've already seen I have a feeling the real you is pretty amazing. How about both of us get to know him at the same time?"

He flashed his shy smile, but nodded to agree. "I work in a

job I don't love even though my trust fund is large enough that I wouldn't have to work a day in my life if I didn't want to. My current circle of friends are superficial people who never call when I'm away and probably wouldn't miss me if I didn't come back. I live on the road and have never lived more than three years in any one place my entire life. And my parents don't know how to talk to me. How's that for a start?"

"It's good. Where were you born?"

"Sydney, Australia."

"Really? Cool. How did you get the scar across your eyebrow?"

He rubbed his finger across the scar. "Is it that noticeable?"

"No. I just have an eye for interesting details."

"When we were little, my brother and I were playing hide and seek and he ran into the house. I sprinted around the corner to chase him and smacked into the closed sliding glass door at full speed. I was so stunned I just lay down on the deck and stared up at the sky. Cody opened the door and laughed until he saw blood gushing down my face. He pressed his hand on the gash to try to make the bleeding stop, so we were both covered in blood when our nanny found us. She started screaming hysterically in Spanish because she thought he tried to kill me." He chuckled. "That part was funny, but it literally scarred me for life."

"It makes you unique. I like it." As we ate, I thought about more questions to ask him—questions that would help both of us to get to know him better. "What's your all-time favourite movie?"

"*Meatballs.*" He opened a Perrier and took a sip.

"Is that the old summer camp one?"

"Yeah. I like all Bill Murray movies. He's funny."

"You're weird. I thought my taste in movies was outdated." There was a bar of dark chocolate in the picnic basket, so I smiled and opened the wrapper to share a square with him. "What was your favourite story as a child?"

He lay back on the blanket and closed his eyes to bask in the sun. "*The Velveteen Rabbit*."

"That was about a toy that became real because it was loved, right?" I asked, trying to remember the story.

Mason shrugged. "I don't really remember the story, just that I liked it and I made my mom read it every night for almost a year. My brother liked *Pippy Longstocking* for some reason." He chuckled as he remembered.

I rolled over onto my stomach and rested my cheek on my folded arms. "What is your favourite memory of your brother?"

He thought for a while, then he sat up and smiled. "We were both scared to sleep in our own beds, so after my mom turned out the light, I would either sneak into his bed or he would sneak into mine. We would read books or play with toys with a flashlight under the covers until we fell asleep."

"That's very cute."

He got quiet and I could tell he was thinking about something that was upsetting him. "I've never told anyone this before." He licked his bottom lip and looked away as if he'd changed his mind about sharing. I waited and eventually he looked back at me and said, "I thought it was my fault he got cancer."

"What do you mean?"

"We were eleven and he hadn't being feeling well for a couple of weeks. My mom told me I wasn't allowed to sleep in his bed when he was sick and I still snuck in every night without her knowing. One night we were messing around, wrestling and jumping on the bed in a competition to see who could touch the ceiling the most times in a minute. I let him win, but afterwards he got really tired, so I lay next to him. In the middle of the night he couldn't breathe and his nose was bleeding. I got my mom and he was rushed to the hospital and diagnosed. They treated him with chemotherapy and radiation, but he died five years later. I was lying next to him in his bed when that happened, too."

I sat up and crossed my legs again. "It wasn't your fault he got cancer."

He shook his head. "I know, but I thought it was."

I completely understood the pain he was feeling, so I reached over and squeezed his hand. "Mason, I'm going to tell you something that very few people know about me. It's weird, which is why only the people I trust know."

His expression creased, both curious and apprehensive.

"Last night when we were at your house and I zoned out, it wasn't epilepsy. I get intuitive visions sometimes."

"Like a psychic?"

"The books call it clairvoyant. My grandmother's grandmother was able to do it too. It's like a really strong gut instinct accompanied by flashes of images. Lately my visions have become more frequent and more accurate but when I was younger I usually didn't know what they meant until it was too late." I glanced at his expression to gauge how much of a whack job he thought I was. He seemed open to the possibility, so I continued, "I know what it feels like to wish you could change the past. I also know what it feels like to blame yourself for someone dying. And maybe that was the connection you saw hidden behind my expression when we first met in high school." I took a deep breath before continuing. "I saw my dad's car accident before it happened. In the vision I couldn't see the driver's face, so I didn't stop him from going to visit my mom in Vancouver that day. He'd still be alive if I had figured it out in time."

Mason's eyes met mine.

"It would have been my choice that my dad didn't die. But since he did, I wish I could have at least been with him in his last moments. That way the last thing he would have felt was my love." Tears blinked out and rolled down my cheeks. "The cancer killed your brother. You didn't. He maybe would have died that night when he couldn't breathe if you hadn't been there. And lying with him near the end to make sure he wasn't alone when it was time for him to go was the most precious thing you could have done for him. He was lucky to have you there."

He nodded and stared off at the view as he processed. "Thank you for saying that," he said softly.

"Thank you for sharing with me."

I sat up on my knees and wrapped my arms around his shoulders to give him a hug, then we both lay back and watched the clouds float by as the sound of the water and the songbirds lulled us into a peaceful state. We were definitely connected on a level that I couldn't explain. Maybe it was Cody and my dad smiling down. Or maybe it was just two people who, once you got past the surface differences, were very similar at the core. Whatever ended up happening at the end of the summer, I would never forget Mason.

# CHAPTER 17

After our picnic, Mason dropped me off at the Inn and then headed down to Vancouver to get some work done. I took over for my granddad at the front desk for the rest of the afternoon. Because the weather was so gorgeous all of the guests were out enjoying outdoor activities, which meant it was quiet enough for me to hang out in the library, sketching.

Jim had already returned before Mason dropped me off after lunch, but Trevor wasn't home. If Trevor had been hurt badly on the search Jim would have come over to tell me, so that was a relief. But it made me wonder where Trevor was and whether he had changed his mind about our talk. When he still hadn't returned by dinner time I texted him to ask when he wanted to meet. He didn't respond.

I sat out on the deck and read, partly to enjoy the summer evening and partly to watch for him to come home. At ten o'clock, I gave up and went to my room. I texted him one more time: *Are you okay?* then I fell asleep waiting for his reply.

At one-thirty in the morning, a knock at my bedroom door woke me up. I was super-groggy as I got out of bed, stumbled to the door, and opened it. It was dark in my room and bright in the hallway, so I had to squint as the light flooded in. At first, I didn't know who was standing propped up against the doorframe. I blinked and let my eyes adjust. The entire side of his face was purple and his eye was swollen almost shut. "Trevor? Oh my God," I gasped. "What happened?"

"Hey." The smell of liquor seeped out of him.

"Are you drunk?"

"A little bit," he slurred and shifted as if his balance was off.

"What happened to your face? I told you to be careful."

"I was careful. But I fell. It was an accident. Never mind. I'm fine. Sort of. Don't distract me or I'll forget the things I need to say to you." He held up one finger and tried, somewhat unsuccessfully, to point at me. "I came over earlier to talk to you. You were gone. Kailyn said you were on a date with Cartwright again. And I want to tell you." He paused and glanced up at the ceiling. "I can't remember exactly what I was going to say, but you should know I have always loved you and I would never let anything bad happen to you. Never. Your happiness is the only thing I have ever cared about. Ever. So if Cartwright makes you happy I won't stand in your way. If he hurts you, I'll kill him. You look hot by the way." He pointed at my tank top and underwear ensemble, then limped down the hallway holding his side.

"Trevor. Wait." I ran after him and grabbed his elbow, which made him almost fall over. He had to brace himself against the wall. "What are you doing? You said you wanted to talk, but you show up pissed drunk and barely making any sense?"

"I came earlier. I made sense then. You were gone. With him. You should be with him. No chance, for me. I tried to make the pain go away. It's worse." His breath caught in his throat as he struggled to stand upright. "I don't feel good."

"Come in. You can lie down."

"Rich is better."

"What? That doesn't even make any sense."

126

"And I think I'm going to throw up." He turned and pushed out the exit door into the parking lot.

After I recovered from the shock of what he said, I rushed back into my room and searched for my phone. Sophie was a night owl, so there was a good probability she would be awake, but even if she wasn't it was an important enough dilemma to wake her for. There was a message from Mason already on my phone: *What u said about my brother today meant the world to me. Thank you.*

My heart felt weird, like it was cramping, and a lump swelled in my throat. Why did everything need to be so complicated? Obviously I attracted it into my life somehow, but I didn't want to anymore. I wanted things to be simple and easy. For once. When Sophie answered I was surprisingly calm, which made me worry that maybe I was going into real shock. "He said he loved me."

"Who? Trevor?"

"He was drunk and he came over. He said, 'I have always loved you.' I think I know what it means, but what do you think it means? Does he mean I love you like a kid sister and I don't want you to get hurt, or I-love-you-love-you like I'm going to break up with my girlfriend for you?"

"Jesus. I can't keep up. I still haven't even heard how your date with Mason went last night. What else did Trevor say?"

"Um, he said my happiness is all he cares about, if Mason makes me happy he won't stand in my way, that he'll kill Mason if he hurts me, etcetera. Oh yeah, and before he left he said, 'You look hot'."

"Were you sweaty or wearing something nice?"

"Neither. I was in my underwear and a tank top."

She laughed. "He definitely meant I-love-you-love-you and he's going to break up with his girlfriend for you if you want him to."

"What should I do?"

127

"Go talk to him and tell him that you love him too."

"What about Mason?"

"What about Mason? You went on one date."

"Three dates, two of which were amazing. He took me on a picnic today and we have a lot in common. I like him. I'm confused."

"You weren't supposed to fall for Mason, you dork. He's just a means to an end."

"That sounds so cold. He's a real person who has real feelings."

"It's simple. Sweet, hot guy you've loved for thirteen years, or sweet, hot guy you've gone on a few dates with."

I thought about Sophie's oversimplification for a second, then said, "Trevor's drunk. Should I wait until the morning and tell him when he's sober?"

"I wouldn't wait."

"Okay, I'm going over. I'll call you tomorrow. Thanks."

I hung up and looked out my window. His bedroom light was on, so I put on yoga pants and a sweat top, then ran out of the Inn and across the parking lot. I took two steps at a time up to the Mavertys' porch and slid my finger along the top of the door frame to find their spare key.

The lights were off in the living room and kitchen, so I snuck up the stairs. Hopefully Jim wasn't awake. If he thought I was an intruder he would take me down, no questions asked. I knocked softly on Trevor's door. There was no answer, so I knocked again and opened it a crack. He was sprawled on the bed, stomach down, still wearing his jacket and boots. "Trevor," I whispered. "Trev," I said more loudly before stepping into the room and closing the door behind me.

He moved a little and groaned, but he didn't wake up. I sat on the edge of his bed and watched him. His eyebrows were creased together with stress or pain. The bruised part of his cheek was on the pillow, which he would probably regret in the morning. I ran my palm down the side of his face and along the angle of his jaw. It was rough, as if he hadn't shaved in a couple of days.

His room hadn't changed too much since we were little. We used to play in his room all the time and I was familiar with most everything in it. His old red baseball cap was sitting on the shelf. I put it on and wandered around. The leather jacket he leant me was hanging from the closet doorknob. The frame on his desk had a photo of me in it. I was about fifteen and sitting on the railing of the deck at the Inn. The shot caught me mid-laugh and it seemed as if I didn't know the picture was being taken. There was also a picture of Kailyn, him, and me in a rowboat when we were all really little. I had sent him that photo while he was in Europe. It was adorable and it brought back good memories from when my dad was still alive. Memories like Trevor and me helping baby ducks cross the highway; him putting a band-aid on my knee after I fell off my bike; my mom hugging him when he was about ten because he made a clay picture frame at school and gave it to her for Mother's Day; him throwing rocks at my bedroom window so we could sneak out at night to watch a meteor shower; us running in the forest. We raced to get to the top of the mountain before the sun rose. We got there at exactly the same time and watched in awe as the sun flooded the valley with warm light. It was beautiful.

Trevor moved a little and winced, but he didn't wake up, so I took off his boots for him, kissed him on the forehead, and left.

# CHAPTER 18

I couldn't fall asleep at first because I was rehearsing in my mind what I wanted to say to Trevor. Every couple of hours, I woke up and checked the clock. The night seemed to take forever to pass. At five o'clock, I sprung out of bed, showered, and spent a little extra time on my hair and outfit.

The guests all came and went for breakfast with no sign of Trevor. His truck was still out front, so I figured he was either hung over or in too much pain from whatever happened to him on the rescue. I didn't mind waiting. It would go better if he wasn't irritable and grumpy.

The hours passed and I decided that if he didn't come over by three o'clock I would go check on him and make sure he was okay. At noon, Kailyn burst into the lobby as I was sorting the accounts receivable for the Inn. Her face was flushed and her fists were balled at her side.

"Kailyn, what's wrong?"

"You are very mean, Derian. Trevor ran away on his motorcycle because you hurt his feelings."

"What do you mean? He left?"

"He ran away forever and it's your fault. You're being a bad girl because you go on dates with Mason Cartwright. I don't love you anymore." She swung the door open and rushed out.

"Kailyn," I yelled through the open door. She stormed across the parking lot, stomped up their porch steps, and slammed the door behind her.

Talking to her when she was angry never went well. I decided to let her cool off before I attempted it. Sophie called for an update, so I headed to my bedroom to talk in privacy. There was a note on my floor that must have been slipped under the door. I picked it up as I said to Sophie, "It didn't happen." I tossed the note on my desk.

"Why not? Did you chicken out?"

"No. He was passed out when I went there last night. And Kailyn just informed me that he took off on his bike, possibly permanently. So there goes my chance." I put a sweater on and zipped the front, then walked back to my desk and picked up the note. It was from Trevor.

*Deri,*
*I'm taking off for a while to give you space. I apologize if I said anything last night that I shouldn't have. I can't remember that well.*

*Trev*

"Deri," Sophie said louder to get my attention.

"What? Sorry. I wasn't listening. Trevor left me a note that I just read."

"What does it say?"

"Goodbye, basically." I sighed and threw the paper on my desk. "Is it all right if I come over to hang out? I need to not be here right now."

"Absolutely. Doug is leaving soon. Come over whenever you want. I live for this type of drama."

"Thanks. I'm on my way."

After I hung up, I headed to the library to talk to my granddad. He was reading in his armchair, so I sat on the couch across from him. "I know I've been going out a lot, but will you be okay if I go out again this afternoon?"

He nodded and took his glasses off to study my face. "Do you have another date with Mason?"

"No. I need a break from dating for a while. I'm going to Sophie's. I'll probably sleep over. Is there anything you need me to do before I go?"

"Don't worry about me and the Inn. Alan and Paula are eager to do as much as possible. You should take it easy and enjoy your last summer here. Do you want to borrow the car?"

"Sure. If you don't mind. How is your condo in Squamish coming along?"

"Good. The construction is on schedule. I should be able to move in by the end of August. Before you leave for Toronto, we can move your furniture into the second bedroom. That way you will be all set up to visit anytime you like."

"That sounds really nice. But Toronto is still up in the air."

"Really? I thought you decided for sure." Although he had never outwardly expressed any reluctance about me going to U of T, he seemed pleased to find out that I might not go.

"I'm confused right now."

"Well, Squamish would be quite the commute every day, but you are welcome to live with me in the apartment full time. Not that you probably want to live with an old man. It's an option, though, if living with your mom goes as well as I imagine it will."

I laughed because he didn't comment on my relationship with my mom that often. "Thank you. I might need to take you up on that offer."

I stood and kissed his cheek. "If you need me to come back from Sophie's, just call."

He patted my hand. "Drive safe."

"I will. Love you."

I grabbed his car keys from the desk and left out the lobby door. Before I started the engine, I texted Trevor: *Let me know you're safe.* He didn't respond.

I drove into Squamish and parked a few houses down from Sophie's. Doug was sitting in his car across the street, slumped over the steering wheel. I walked up and knocked on the driver-side window. He rolled his head and his eyes attempted to focus on me.

"Are you okay?" I shouted through the glass.

He frowned and squinted as if the brightness of the clear blue sky hurt his brain. I opened the door and rested my palm on his forehead. He was cold and sweaty.

"What's wrong? Are you sick?"

"No. I'm fine." He was shaking.

"I don't think you are. Let's get you back inside."

"No."

"Well, you can't drive. You look horrible."

He pushed my hand away. "I don't want Sophie to see me like this."

"Like what? What's wrong with you?"

"Nothing."

"There's something wrong with you."

After a hesitation, he held up my granddad's prescription bottle and shook it. It was empty. He didn't say anything. He just rested his forehead on the steering wheel.

"Do you want me to take you to a medical clinic to get more?"

"They won't give me more," he mumbled.

"Why? If your back still hurts they should give you something for it."

"My back doesn't still hurt." He popped his head up and looked at me as if he got a bright idea. "They'll give some to you. You can tell them you're in pain for something and they'll give you a prescription."

I frowned and let everything sink in. "So, you don't need

painkillers for pain, you need painkillers because you're addicted."

He tilted his head and looked at me in an apologetic way. "Will you help me get more?"

"Jesus. Shove over." I pushed him into the passenger seat and slid into the driver's seat. "Give me the keys."

He abruptly opened the passenger door and leaned out to puke on the sidewalk. He heaved a few more times, then sat up straight and closed the door. "Are you going to help me?"

"Yes," I said and patted his jacket pockets for the keys.

"Promise you won't tell Sophie."

"You know I can't make that kind of promise." I started his car and drove down the street.

"Please, don't tell her. She'll leave me if she finds out I'm hooked. If you get me another bottle right now, I promise I'll get clean."

"I'm not getting you more."

"You have to, Deri. I feel like I'm dying."

He was shaking and sweating. I shook my head and drove out of the neighbourhood, then turned the corner onto the street his apartment was on. I parked and basically dragged him by the leather of his jacket to the elevator. I used the key to open the door to his suite and helped him take his boots and jacket off. "Go lie down." I put my purse down and called Sophie. Doug watched me as I waited for her to answer. His eyes pleaded with me. "Hey, Soph. Something came up at the Inn and my granddad needs my help. I'm not going to be able to come over."

Doug mouthed, *Thank you.*

"Okay, yeah. Thanks. I'll call you tomorrow." I hung up and stared at him. He was half-buckled over as if he was going to puke again. "You owe me. Go lie down while I figure out what to do."

"You could at least get me some Tylenol." He paced around the apartment for a minute, then went into the kitchen and opened a cupboard. He pulled out bottles of vitamins and threw them on the floor until the cupboard was empty.

"Doug, settle down."

He stormed across the living room towards the bathroom and chucked things around. His laptop was open on his desk, so I sat down to search painkiller addictions and withdrawal. "Deri! Just go to the damn pharmacy and get me some Tylenol."

"No."

He stood in the doorway to the bathroom and glared at me. "Then you might as well leave if you're not going to help me."

"No. I'm not leaving and I'm not getting you anything. Just stop talking while I figure out what to do."

"I know what you need to do. You need to get me some fucking pills."

Startled by his tone and language, my mouth dropped open. He had never spoken to me that way before.

He cringed. "Sorry. Sorry. Sorry. I didn't mean to swear at you. Sorry." He pulled at tufts of his hair and paced around.

"It's okay. Just try to breathe. It's going to be okay." I attempted to sound calm, but I wasn't.

He bolted back into the bathroom and vomited. I got up and stood in the doorway to make sure he was okay. Eventually, he stopped puking and turned to sit against the tub. His hair was soaked in sweat and he trembled. "Deri, I think I'm dying. My heart feels like it's out of control."

"I'll take you to the hospital."

"No. They'll put me in rehab. The band needs me. Please, just get me some sort of painkiller."

He started crying and it slayed me to see a person I considered invincible look so vulnerable. I sat on the floor next to him and wrapped my arms around his shoulders. "Do you want to feel better temporarily or do you want to get better?"

He leaned into my hug. "I want to get better, but I don't think I can. It kills."

"I'll help you. We can do it together. Okay?"

A key turned in the lock and the door to the apartment opened.

I assumed it was Sophie. Instead, Trevor appeared at the bathroom door and frowned as he took in the scene of Doug and me embracing on the floor.

# CHAPTER 19

Doug abruptly pulled away from my hug and aimed more puke into the toilet. Struggling, he pulled himself up to lean his elbows on the edge of the bowl. In between retches he mumbled, "Sorry."

I knelt behind him and rubbed his back as he hung his head. "It's okay."

Trevor assessed the seriousness of the situation quickly and asked, "What can I do to help?"

I pointed in the direction of the living room. "I started a search on his laptop to find out about OxyContin withdrawal. You could search some more to see if we need to take him to the hospital."

"No," Doug moaned. "No hospital. I don't want anybody to know."

Trevor turned and walked down the hall to the living room. The computer chair squeaked as he sat down. Doug crawled on his knees to the base of the sink and held on to the counter to attempt to stand. I helped him to his feet and he washed out his mouth.

"I think I need to lie down."

"Okay." I stretched his arm across my shoulders and propped his weight against mine to guide him to his bedroom. He flopped down on the mattress and closed his eyes, but not in a restful way. It seemed more like he was bracing from the pain. Worried,

I joined Trevor in the living room to check if there was something more we should be doing.

Trevor leaned back in the computer chair and tilted his head back to look at me. "How is he?"

"He's in bed. But I don't think he'll be able to sleep."

"How long has he been taking OxyContin?"

"Three months."

He read through a medical article online and then texted Murphy to ask what the paramedics normally do. He read the response, then said, "He'll probably be okay detoxing here. But we should monitor his vitals. Murphy is on shift tonight. We can call him if we need him to come over." He turned in the chair to face me. "Where's Sophie?"

"Doug doesn't want her to know."

"You have to tell her. How would you feel if it was the other way around?"

He was right, so I sighed and called her. "Hey Soph, you need to come to Doug's place."

"Why? What's wrong?"

"He's sick. Just come over. I'll explain everything when you get here."

"I'll be right there."

She hung up and I looked at Trevor—partly angry at him for leaving without talking to me first, but I was mostly relieved he wasn't actually gone. "I didn't expect to see you here. Kailyn made it sound like you took off."

"I couldn't leave right away. It's been really busy and a lot of the Search and Rescue guys are on holidays. I didn't want to leave my dad short-handed. Doug said I could crash here."

"So, you're still leaving?"

He shrugged. "That's the plan."

"Where are you going?"

"Probably through the Rockies—Banff, Lake Louise. Or maybe north into Yukon."

I shook my head, hurt that he didn't even care where he went and had no reservations about leaving on a trip that big without bothering to tell me to my face. "Just so you know, when someone texts you asking whether you are okay, the decent thing to do is respond with yes, I'm fine, thanks for asking."

"I was on top of a mountain without service. What did you expect me to do?"

Not buying that as his only excuse, I went into the kitchen and poured myself a glass of water in an attempt to stay calm. He watched me cautiously as if he knew I was about to pick a fight so everything would be laid on the table. The bruising on his face had turned a deeper blue and his eye was still almost swollen shut, so I launched my first blow to get the argument going. "You look like shit."

"Yeah, well high-angle rescue and distractions don't go well together."

"What distractions?" I placed the glass on the counter and crossed my arms, prepared to completely get into it with him. "Girlfriend problems?"

He exhaled stressfully and rubbed the back of his neck before he said, "Lindy and I aren't going out, if that's what you're refer-ring to."

"Why? Did she break up with you because she found out you kissed me?"

"No." His eyes met mine, maybe remembering the kiss or maybe thinking about what he wanted to say next. "We only went out a few times. It was never serious."

Not entirely disarmed by that answer, I stepped into the living room and leaned against the wall by the door. "If that's true, why did she sleep over?"

"My dad and I went out on a rescue. When we got back, it was late. She didn't feel comfortable driving on the highway alone at night, so my dad invited her to stay. She slept in his bed and he slept on the couch."

"Why didn't you just tell me that?"

"I tried." He leaned forward and his voice rose. "You literally slammed the door in my face. And then you took off in Cartwright's helicopter."

"Right. Sorry about that." I tucked my hair behind my ears and slid my back down the wall to sit on the floor. "Why did she show up at your house unannounced in the first place?"

"I lent her money last term. She was just paying me back."

My eyes rolled because that seemed like an unlikely story. "She could have just e-transferred or mailed you a cheque. But instead she drove all the way up to Britannia Beach. Does she still like you?"

"Does it matter?"

"I don't know. Does it?" I challenged, and then hugged my knees into my chest.

He stood and moved to sit on the arm of the couch, facing me. "She was interested in me and pursued me since September. She would show up at the library when I was studying or join my friends at lunch without asking and eventually became a part of my social circle. I needed a date for a faculty dinner once and she took me as a guest to a friend's wedding once. I was never into her."

"Why not? She's breathtakingly beautiful."

"Because she's not you."

He stood and walked over to slide his back down the wall and sit next to me on the floor. After a deep breath he rested his hand, palm up on his thigh, so I would hold it—like a truce.

"Deri, you are the only person I have ever been into. Within the first few minutes of meeting you I knew you were someone special. As we got older, I realized just how incredibly rare a connection like ours is. You shared all my interests like a best friend, you knew everything about me like a sister, and you took my breath away like my dream girl—all at the same time. By the time I was fifteen I was hopelessly in love with you." His fingers squeezed around mine. He turned his head and our eyes locked. "And I still am."

My eyebrows angled together and my breathing halted temporarily as I took a second to replay what he said and to make sure I heard right. "Seriously?"

He smiled and sparks of energy scattered across my skin. "You've always known I love you."

"I knew you cared, but I was confused because you never asked me out. Why didn't you want to date?"

"I did, I just thought it would be better for you to have the experiences of dating other guys so you wouldn't always wonder if there was something better out there." He clenched his eyes shut for a second as if he regretted that decision. "My plan was to ask you out at your graduation, but you were excited about your Europe trip and I didn't want to interfere with that. Then when you got back, Mason beat me to it."

"You let him beat you."

He shrugged as if it was true. "Mason can give you a lot of things I can't. It's better if you find out now what you really want instead of getting trapped in a life you resent."

"I'm not your mom. You're the one who's like your mom. You take off every time things get even a little bit complicated."

"I'm nothing like her." The tendons in his neck tightened from the comparison. "You know I always come back."

That was true. He always came back. "But you leave without talking or trying to solve things."

"I'm sorry. I wanted to give you space to think and figure things out on your own." He was quiet for a while and stared at our intertwined hands. Then he sighed. "I didn't want you to end up like my mom did and wake up one day wondering if I really was the right one, or the convenient one."

I squeezed his hand between both of mine. "Weren't you worried that when you encouraged me to date other people there was a very good chance I might actually develop feelings for one of them?"

He shrugged. "I'd rather you figure it out now. Why? Do you like Cartwright?"

I thought about if for a while, then answered honestly, "Yes. He's really amazing." I turned to face Trevor and sat cross-legged next to his hip. "But I love you."

The side of his mouth lifted in an adorable grin. He started to speak but then something smashed in Doug's bedroom and startled both of us.

We both got up and rushed down the hall.

# CHAPTER 20

Doug stood hunched over in front of the mirror in his bedroom. It was shattered and his right hand was bleeding in streams down his forearm. "Get out!" he shouted at us.

"You're bleeding. Let me help you," I said.

"Unless you're going to get me what I need, I don't want you here. Take Maverty with you. I want to be alone." He sat on the edge of the bed and clenched his arms against his abdomen as if he was having bad cramps. He groaned and rocked his upper body back and forth towards his knees.

I glanced over my shoulder at Trevor. His eyebrows angled together. "Maybe I should call the ambulance."

There was a knock at the door, so Trevor turned and went to answer. Doug glanced at me and blinked slowly as if his eyelids were too heavy. When he heard Sophie's voice, his expression contorted into rage. He grabbed me by both shoulders and shoved me across the room. I smashed into the dresser and landed in a heap on the floor. "Bitch. I told you not to call her."

I wanted to say something to defend myself but the air had been knocked out of my lungs. The only sound I could muster was a weird wheezing. Blood dripped onto the floor from a cut on my forehead. I touched the spot above my eye and felt warm stickiness.

Trevor and Sophie both raced into the room and stood with their mouths hanging open once they saw that I was bleeding. Trevor was about to move in to restrain Doug, but I knew it would be ugly if it turned into a fight, so I held my hand up to stop him. "I'm okay."

I slowly stood and made eye contact with Doug. He widened his stance in a posture like a cornered animal. I took a slow step towards him and waited to see how he was going to react. His eyes darted between each of us. I exhaled and stood motionless to let him settle down. His muscles were still rigid and sweat ran down the sides of his face. Holding my breath, I inched closer and waited. Eventually his expression softened and he relaxed enough to let me put my arms around him. I turned my face and rested my cheek on his chest. His heart bounced off his ribs in a crazy rhythm.

He inhaled deeply and hugged me back. "I'm sorry, Deri. I didn't mean to hurt you."

"I know. It's going to be okay."

Once he knew I was safe, Trevor called Murphy. He showed up ten minutes later with his paramedic partner to examine Doug. They said the worst part of the detox was probably over and gave us instructions on how to take care of him. Murphy had to go back to work, but he said to call him if there were any problems and he'd come back.

"Thanks Murph," Sophie said and then hugged each of us. "I'll stay with him while he sleeps. You guys can head home too if you want."

"I was planning to crash here tonight anyway," Trevor said. "I'll sleep out on the couch in case you need help with anything."

She glanced wide-eyed in my direction in what I assumed was her way of encouraging me to take advantage of the golden opportunity. Then she went to be with Doug in the bedroom.

After Murphy left, Trevor sat down on the couch next to me and exhaled. "How's your head?"

Murphy had cleaned it so there wasn't any blood but it was swollen. I touched it and it hurt, but I said, "Fine."

He got up and headed to the kitchen to open the freezer. He scooped some crushed ice into a sandwich bag and brought it back to place it above my eye. "Did Doug call you? Is that why you were here?"

"No. I was on my way over to Sophie's and found him slumped over in his car." I sat cross-legged on the cushion and faced him. I stared for a while because he looked different to me after officially declaring his love. "Did it feel weird for you to kiss me after being friends for so long?"

"No." He sat back and stretched his legs out. "It felt exactly how I always imagined it would."

"And how was that?"

He smiled and glanced at me. "Awesome."

My breath hitched in my throat for a second before the grin spread across my face.

"Did it feel weird to you?"

"No." I shook my head slowly, still grinning, as I remembered the kiss. "It felt perfectly natural, like destiny." I tossed the bag of melting ice into a mug on the coffee table, then planted my hands on the middle cushion and shifted onto my knees to crawl closer. "I don't suppose you would be interested in doing it again?" I touched the end of my nose to his and smiled.

His hand slid up to rest on the side of my jaw and he gently drew my face towards his. "I would love to kiss you again, but you need to know that you have options—guys like Mason, going to school in Toronto, travelling, or whatever else you might want to experience. I don't want to tell you what to do and I don't want to stand in your way of anything. Live the life you want."

I nodded and let it all sink in. "I don't need more life experiences to know that everything about you complements who I am and makes me whole. What more could there be out there than that?"

He didn't answer, and it was hard to tell if he didn't have a counter-argument or if he was distracted by my hand running up his thigh. Either way, I was winning the debate.

"I just want you to do what feels right," he finally said.

I knew I had options, but my first choice would always be him. It was an easy choice. I gazed into his eyes and inched closer. "You feel right."

After flashing me a drop-me-to-my-knees-begging type of smile he leaned in to kiss me tenderly along my jaw line. Then he paused just below my ear and let his lips hover close to my skin for an excruciatingly exciting moment. He kissed his way towards my mouth and when he slid his tongue along the surface of my lower lip, tingles shot up my spine. A warm sensation radiated from his lips and pulsated through me with each beat of my heart—like our souls were fusing.

I moved and swung my leg over to straddle his thighs. His hands rested on my hips to pull me in closer, but his jaw muscles tensed into a serious expression. "I love you, Deri, but I want you to be sure about this. It would kill me if you made your choices for me and ended up unhappy."

I clutched his neck and leaned in to speak into his ear. "I am sure."

Our lips locked and every moment of closeness we'd ever shared came rushing back to me. The memories took my breath away—the meaningful grazes of my hand, the secrets and wishes we had whispered, every knowing glance from across the room, the comforting hugs, reassuring forehead kisses, encouraging pep-talks, the way his confidence and bravery always surrounded me in a fiercely protective embrace, and how we called each other on our bullshit with an intensity that only someone who loves you unconditionally can get away with. I loved him so much.

He moved to lay me back on the cushion and pulled his shirt

off. His body was so incredibly hot I had to remind myself to breathe. My gaze wandered across his broad shoulders before focusing back on his face. He leaned forward to place one hand on either side of me, then slowly lowered his body and hovered over mine as if he was doing a push-up. The anticipation was killing me, so I dug my fingers into his back and pulled him down until our chests pressed together. Clutching his hair, I kissed him hard. And I knew without a doubt that his lips were the only lips I wanted to kiss for the rest of my life.

I ran my hands up his abs, careful to avoid his bruised ribs. His breathing got heavier as my palms caressed his chest. His gaze didn't break contact with mine and something even more intense than the physical touch transferred between us. My back arched as the sensation coursed through my veins. He leaned forward to kiss my throat and his hand trailed along my skin from my waist to my bra, generating heat as it moved.

When my breath became more rapid and my touch more eager, he hesitated and said, "Do you think maybe we should go on a proper date?"

"That would be nice," I hooked my finger under his chin to draw him close for a kiss. "This is nice, too, though."

"This is more than nice," he said. "But maybe we should dial it back. I don't want our first time together to be on Doug's couch."

I rolled my head to the side and took in the environment—a nineteen-year-old rocker's crash pad. "I guess it isn't exactly how I imagined it."

Trevor slid over onto his side next to me and bent his elbow to prop his head up. "How did you imagine it?"

My eyes clenched and my cheeks heated up. "You're going to laugh. It's sort of weird."

He laughed. "Like kinky weird?"

"No." I slapped his chest. "You have to promise not to laugh."

He made a motion to cross his heart with his finger.

I inhaled and released the air slowly to stave off the embarrassment. "For a very long time I have had a fantasy that you and I would sneak out onto the beach together at night. We would lie down on a blanket to gaze up at the stars and listen to the waves lapping against the shore. You would lean over to kiss me, then, all slow and sexy, bathed in the moonlight, it would happen really naturally and beautifully."

He didn't laugh. He stared at me with the most sincere and gentle expression of love I had ever seen. "Then that's how it will happen."

Everything felt like a dream, only it was real. He was right beside me. His muscles were holding me tight. His heat was keeping me warm. His kiss was caressing my skin. I was ridiculously happy.

We were asleep on the couch, cuddled in each other's arms, when the sound of the toilet flushing woke me up. Sophie walked into the living room and leaned her elbows on the back of the couch, grinning. "Well, well, well. What do we have going on here?" she asked and reached down to muss up my already mussed hair even more. Trevor rolled over and groaned because she turned on the lamp.

"What's it look like?" I said and waved my hand to shoo her away.

She didn't shoo. She sat in the armchair and crossed her feet on the coffee table, fully intending to give me the gears. "It looks like Trevor Maverty and Derian Lafleur are sleeping together. Fi. Na. Ly."

"Shouldn't you be with Doug?" I motioned vehemently with my head towards the bedroom and pleaded with my eyes.

"He's asleep. I'm not tired." Her eyebrows rose with amusement because she knew it would drive me insane if she lingered on purpose. "I think we should talk about this." She pointed in a swirly motion to indicate that the *this* she was referring to was Trevor and me.

Trevor chuckled, then sat up and handed me my shirt. He went to the kitchen to get a glass of water and asked if we wanted anything.

"I'll have a beer," Sophie said.

He tossed her one as his phone buzzed. It was the Search and Rescue ringtone so he checked it. He looked torn but said, "I've got to go."

"What's wrong?"

He put his shirt back on. "Some teens didn't return from a hike. Are you going to stay here or head back to Britannia?"

"She's staying here," Sophie answered for me as she twisted the cap off her beer.

I shrugged to agree. I didn't want him to leave, but, more importantly, I didn't want what happened between us to be a one-time thing before he followed through on his plans to disappear to the Rockies or the Yukon or wherever. To check where we stood I asked, "See you at breakfast?"

"Yeah." He bent down to kiss my forehead. "Save me a muffin." He turned to leave and said, "See ya, Soph."

"Byyyyye," she sang. Then, as soon as the door shut behind him, she put the beer down and launched herself towards the couch to tackle and tickle me. "I told you it was going to happen this summer. I want details. Start talking."

# CHAPTER 21

In the morning, I woke up to the smell of coffee. Sophie was in Doug's kitchen. "Morning," I croaked with a raspy voice. His couch was not that comfortable. "How's Doug feeling?"

"Good, apparently. He's in the shower right now, but then he's going to start packing." She reached into the fridge to get the carton of cream, then slammed the door shut.

"Packing for what?"

"He got a call from a band that needs a drummer for their recording sessions in LA. Tomorrow."

"Really? That's awesome. Is he feeling well enough, though?"

She shrugged and threw two slices of bread in the toaster oven. "I guess so."

"You don't seem that happy."

"I'm happy for him, but it sucks for our band and it sucks for our relationship. I'm going to tell him we have to break up."

"What? No. Why?" I got off the couch and moved to sit on the bar stool at the counter.

"The recording session is just the beginning. They want him to tour with them too. If he makes it big with them, our band will fold without him. He thinks he can do both, but if he goes on tour with them, he won't keep playing in a garage band or dating his high-school sweetheart. I'll just be holding him back from his dreams."

"That's not true. He adores you. You guys are soulmates."

She shrugged and then hopped up to sit on the counter next to the sink. "He didn't even want me to be here when he was detoxing. He wanted you to be here."

"He didn't want me here either. I dragged him here and he literally pushed me away."

"The person you love is supposed to be the one person you can tell anything to." She frowned before she reached over to open the toaster oven. "He should have confided in me when he realized he had a problem."

"He was ashamed and afraid he was going to lose you if you saw him like that," I said as I got up to pour myself a glass of juice. "His biggest worry was that you were going to leave him if you found out."

"Well, he should have been more worried about what I would do if he moved to LA and joined a better band." She took a bite of the toast, completely plain. "A drug addiction and living seventeen hundred kilometres away from each other are both fairly significant blows to the relationship."

"You could move there too."

"It's not that easy. I don't have a work visa. And he's not going to want me to follow him around like a groupie. And if I'm not there he'll cheat."

"No he won't. He loves you. He's not the type who would sleep with someone else."

"I never thought he was the type to get hooked on drugs either. People change, obviously. It's better if we break up."

"How can you think about leaving him while he's down? He didn't choose to get hooked. It was a painkiller. The doctor gave it to him."

"GP. Street dealer. What difference does it make? He just proved that he's capable of hiding things from me. I don't want a future of being lied to. And he won't want a future of me holding him back."

"Nobody said that was going to happen. You do realize you're acting just as bad as Trevor by assuming what Doug does or doesn't want. I'm not letting you break up with him pre-emptively."

"It's about what I want too." She sipped her coffee and took another bite of dry toast. "I got an email. An agent who saw us perform in Seattle asked me to audition for a singing part in a play in New York. Off Broadway."

"Are you serious?" I lunged over and hugged her. "That's fantastic. When do you go?"

"Next week. If I get the part, rehearsals start in late August and the show could run for six months or a year depending how well it does. I'd have to move there."

I sat back down, completely stunned. "That is so awesome. Congratulations."

She lifted her eyebrows in an undecided expression. "If Doug's in LA and I'm in New York, things definitely won't work."

"They can work out. You love each other."

"I hate to break it to you, Deri, but sometimes love isn't enough."

That was an unexpected blow. If a relationship as solid as theirs couldn't survive the transition into adulthood, Trevor and I were in trouble.

Noticing that I was reeling from the grim reality, her mood softened. "Sometimes love is enough. What are you going to do? Now that things have heated up with you and Trevor, are you going to stay in Vancouver and go to UBC?"

I sighed and thought about it. "Up until five minutes ago, I wanted to stay to see if things could work with Trevor, but I didn't know you were possibly leaving. Toronto and New York are close. If things are doomed with Trevor and me anyway, maybe I should save myself the heartache. And, honestly, my relationship with my mom is already rocky. I can't even imagine how bad it might get if I actually tried to live with her."

"Things aren't doomed with Trevor. Ignore what I said. You can make it work if you want to. And don't count on me being in New York. I probably won't get the part. It's only an audition."

"You might. You're a really great singer. But if you don't, maybe we could rent an apartment together in Vancouver."

"Yeah, and run a prostitution ring on the side? Do you have any idea how much rent costs in the city? We couldn't afford it with me waitressing and you being a student."

"You could sing or audition for musicals here. Or what about film roles? They shoot in Vancouver all the time. I could get a job and a student loan. Or, I could apply for student housing, I guess." I sighed and braided my hair. "If it were your decision what would you do?"

The water stopped in the shower, so she hopped off the counter. "Which school is better for architecture?"

"They're both excellent."

"Then it boils down to love or money. And maybe climate should be factored in. It's effing cold in Toronto in the winter."

"Well, I need to decide by the end of the week. I have to talk to Trevor first." I sighed and stood. "I should get back to the Inn." I hugged her. "I'm really proud of you, but don't do anything drastic until you find out if you get the part in New York. Doug needs you right now."

"Fine. Thank you for being in charge of my impulse control, yet again."

I laughed. "If you want to talk after he leaves just come over."

"Okay. Thanks."

After I made a quick trip to the bathroom, Sophie walked me to the door and we hugged again. I walked to her house to pick up Granddad's car, then headed back to Britannia Beach. The highway was quiet and the water shimmered in a beautiful way as it reflected the morning light. I couldn't wait to see Trevor again, but I was also nervous that Sophie was right about love not being enough.

The 4Runner was parked in front of their house, his dad's truck wasn't, which at first I thought meant Trevor was home, but then I remembered he was on his bike. Rescues that lasted into the morning meant they were either having trouble finding the hikers or the terrain was too dangerous to attempt in the dark.

I entered the Inn straight through the side door into the kitchen and helped Granddad clean up after the buffet. Then a family wanted to check out, so I met them in the lobby.

The key for room 208 was just sitting on the front desk, as if the guy left without checking out. I pulled up the file on the computer to see if Paula or Alan had processed it and forgot to put the key away, but the check-out wasn't processed. It was weird since he was paid up until Wednesday and the damage deposit was still on file. Whatever, I was glad he was gone.

I checked the family out and then noticed Kailyn's keys on the floor near the desk. I knew they were hers because she had a Kiki key chain that Trevor had carved out of wood for her. I bent over and picked them up, then headed over to return them. The front door to their house was wide open and the TV was on.

I called into the house, "Kiki, are you home?"

There was no answer, so I stepped in and headed to their kitchen.

"Kailyn."

I searched the entire house, upstairs and down. Kailyn wasn't there, so I went back to the Inn and found my granddad. "Have you seen Kailyn?"

"Not since yesterday. She doesn't like that you've been spending so much time with Mason."

"I know. She yelled at me and told me I was being bad. I'm going to look for her. Oh, and by the way, did you see the guy from 208 leave?"

"No. I thought he wasn't supposed to check out until Wednesday."

"He wasn't. The key was on the desk, though."

"Hmm."

Starting to panic a little, I checked my bedroom. Sometimes Kailyn snuck in to try on my makeup. It didn't look like she'd been there. I called her phone as I wandered around, trying to think where else she might have gone. Her phone went to voicemail. My mind jumped to the worst-case scenarios about her being lured away. To calm down, I reminded myself that the last time she ran off, it was because she was mad at me. I'd promised to take her to a movie in Squamish one afternoon. I had totally forgotten and had gone to Vancouver with Sophie instead. Kailyn was so mad at me that she ran away into the forest and got lost. It took Trevor until morning to find her huddled next to a tree crying, but she was safe. Hopefully that's what she had done again.

Jim's Ford F350 passed by the window, so I ran outside and met him at his door. "I can't find Kailyn. She was really mad at me for making Trevor take off and I'm worried she might have run away again. Or worse. She might have gotten a ride with a guest who checked out today."

"The one who made you uncomfortable?"

I nodded, not wanting to accept the possibility, but I had no choice.

In his trademark calmness he said, "I'm sure she's around. I'll take a look." He got out of the truck. "Did you call her phone?"

"Yeah, but I'll try again." I dialled while he looked through the house. Her phone clicked straight to voicemail, so I left another message and met Jim on his porch. "Where is Trevor?"

He glanced across the parking lot towards the highway. "He should have already been here. He left before me."

I ran over to their detached garage and swung the door open. No bike. I texted him and then immediately phoned him when

155

he didn't respond. It went straight to voicemail. My panic ramped up, worried about both of them. Hopefully he just stopped for coffee or to go to Murphy's. Or maybe he went back to check on Doug. Yeah, he probably assumed I'd still be there. Or maybe he changed his mind about us and took off for the Rockies. He wouldn't have done that after what happened between us at Doug's, would he? Maybe he was so tired from being awake most of the night he drove off the road. Oh God. I texted Murphy and Sophie, but neither of them had heard from him either. Maybe he and Kailyn went somewhere together. He wouldn't have left the front door open, though. And he definitely wouldn't have taken her on the back of the bike.

Jim called over to me, "I'm going to check the trails above the upper village. You search the restaurant and shops down here."

I nodded and rushed around asking people, even strangers, if they had seen Kailyn. No one had. I crossed the highway and wandered along the beach. There was no sign of her. I ran back across the highway and just before I reached the front door of the Inn, the vision I'd had before flashed through my mind again: Kailyn laughed with her fists pressed into her cheeks, the way she did when she was excited about something. Trevor's bruised face was tense as he searched for her.

My granddad and the woman who owned the gift shop joined the search. Jim called the Search and Rescue team, which wasn't a good sign. It meant he thought she was really gone.

When Murphy and three other Search and Rescue guys showed up, they had all their gear and they started asking questions and doing things I hadn't thought of. They checked to see if she took a jacket. They figured out, by process of elimination, what kind of shoes she had on. They knew that she took a backpack, but no clothes. She had cleaned out her piggy bank and taken a bunch of granola bars and juice boxes from the pantry.

After they finished going through the house, they tried to call her again, then sent two guys to run the most-used trails to see if she had taken any of them. If she was still on a trail, they could catch up with her.

Two cops and Murphy stepped into the Inn. His massive frame seemed to fill up the entire lobby. "Hey, Deri."

"Hi. Has anyone reached Trevor yet?"

He shook his head and the shorter cop took over. "What is the name of the guest you had concerns about?

"I don't know. He said he didn't have a credit card, but he did. I saw it in his wallet. I asked for his driver's licence and he said he would bring it down later, but he never did."

The two cops exchanged a look like they thought I was useless.

I quickly rattled off everything I could remember about the guy, "He has reddish blond hair that's thin on top and he wears wire-rimmed glasses. He has a scripture tattoo on the inside of his left wrist. He had wanted to stay in Squamish but there were no rooms available, so he came here. He hung out at the casino and he was driving a navy Corolla rental car from Budget." I fumbled through the scrap papers on the desk and found the one I was looking for. "It was a BC licence plate, here's the number." I handed the short guy the paper and then they went outside to call it in from their cruiser.

Murphy said, "Good job, Deri. That will help."

"Do you think he took her?"

He shrugged and said, "Nah," to make me feel better, but I could tell by his expression that he thought it was likely. I felt sick. "Keep trying Trevor," he said before he went back outside.

More guys from Search and Rescue showed up, but still no word from Trevor. I sat outside on the railing of the deck so I could listen to their radio conversations. They were criss-crossing between the trails in case she got turned around.

The cops checked on the rental car and were waiting to get a name they could run through the system. A lot of the things they were doing were above the call of duty because it was for Jim Maverty. Kailyn was twenty-one years old, so she technically had the right to leave without them considering her a missing person. Because of the circumstances, they were doing more than they normally would have.

"Derian," Jim called me over to join him. He was standing in front of his truck with trail maps spread out on a picnic table. "How you holding up, kid?"

"Not great. This is all my fault. She wouldn't have left if I hadn't upset her. I'm so sorry."

"Don't blame yourself. You could just as easily say it was my fault for not being here to keep an eye on her. We could all blame ourselves, but it doesn't do any good. It's better to focus our energy on trying to find her. Unfortunately, there's not much more we can do right now but wait for the police to trace the plate."

"Any word from Trevor?"

"No." He glanced at me as if there were things he wanted to say about that. "He had a pretty bad fall. His head hasn't been in the game lately."

"Sorry. That's my fault, too."

"Well, I'm sure you two will figure it out. You and Trevor have something special that is probably worth working on." He stretched his arm across my shoulder and gave me a quick squeeze. "Just tell him what you want from him and he'll do it, gladly. We Mavertys aren't as complicated as we seem."

I lifted my eyebrows, not convinced that was true. But glad that he thought a future between Trevor and me was worth fighting for.

He grabbed a bottle of water off the picnic table. "Have you had any visions lately that might point us in the right direction?"

"Nothing that would help. I saw Kailyn's face and I knew Trevor was looking for her, but there weren't any specifics about where."

He exhaled tensely and his forehead creased between his eyebrows, just like Trevor. "Give Trevor another call. Okay?"

"Sure." I walked back to the deck, filled with dread. Even Jim was worried. That was bad. What if the guy was a sexual predator? What if he was a serial killer? Trevor would lose it if Kailyn was hurt in any way. I was scared to tell him, but I was more terrified to not know why he hadn't come home. My hands shook so badly, I could barely press the screen to dial his number. My entire body started to tremble and I struggled to keep the phone still against my ear as I waited for him to answer. It rang several times before he finally picked up. "Thank God, Trevor. Are you okay? Why haven't you been answering your phone? We've all been trying to get a hold of you."

"I was riding. I just stopped for gas. What's wrong?"

"Promise you won't freak out?"

His tone became severe as he sensed my panic. "What is it?"

I started to cry. "Don't freak out."

"Derian, just tell me what happened. Is it Kailyn?"

"We can't find her. We don't know if she ran away or if she went with the weird guy who was staying at the Inn."

His motorcycle engine revved and the phone cut out.

# CHAPTER 22

Trevor hadn't said where he was, so I had no idea how long it was going to take him to get back home. I rocked on a deckchair, biting my nails and staring at the initials that Trevor and I had carved into the wood when we were little. We used his Swiss army knife and I carved them because we thought my printing would be neater. TM + DL. My grandma had been really mad when she caught us, but afterwards she realized it was sweet and wouldn't let my granddad paint over it.

I was completely lost in thought and it startled me when Murphy stepped up on the porch. He rested against the railing and stared at me for a while. His expression made it seem as if they had found something that wasn't good. "What is it?" I asked.

"They found out the name on the rental car agreement, but he used a stolen credit card and driver's licence, so they still don't know his real identity. There is a guy wanted on a Canada-wide warrant who meets the description you gave."

"What's he wanted for?"

"Fraud."

"That's good, isn't it? At least he's not wanted for sexual assault or forcible confinement or something."

Murphy shrugged and crossed his arms. "I doubt he would be luring a vulnerable woman for innocent reasons."

I closed my eyes and tipped my head back, wishing I could go back in time and protect her. "Does the car have GPS tracking? Can they find out where he is?"

"RCMP found it abandoned at a gas station in Whistler. They're checking video surveillance to see if Kailyn was with him."

Trevor's motorcycle came flying into the parking lot. He parked, took his helmet off, and rushed over to talk to his dad. Murphy and I crossed the lot to join them. After Jim explained everything that was being done, Trevor took his leather jacket off and hugged me to his side. It was a helpless feeling for all of them because it wasn't the type of search and rescue they could help with.

They all looked at me as if they got the same idea simultaneously.

"What?"

Trevor turned to face me and held me by the shoulders. "It's going to take the police forever to track the guy down. If you can see something it might help us find her faster."

In the past, my visions didn't work that way. I couldn't will them to happen. But maybe the increased frequency also came with increased control. Maybe if I really concentrated I could see more. "I could try."

Jim leaned against his truck, thumbs hooked in the pockets of his jeans. "What if you sit in her room surrounded by her things?"

Desperate to help, I agreed. "Yeah. That's a good idea. I'll try."

Trevor walked with me up to her room. He let me step in the room and he lingered at her door. "I'll leave you alone to let you concentrate."

"I don't know if it will work."

"Don't worry if it doesn't. It's worth a try, though." He stepped in and hugged me to his chest.

161

Hearing how fast his heart was beating I asked, "Where were you when I called? I was worried when I couldn't get a hold of you."

"I forgot one of the extrication packs at the top of the waterfall and had to hike back to get it. I was out of range. I'm sorry I didn't get the call earlier."

"She said I was being a bad girl because I hurt your feelings and made you leave. I'm sorry."

He bent over to whisper into my ear. "It's my fault for taking off, not yours." He kissed my cheek and then left.

I crossed the room and sat on the edge of her mattress, but nothing happened, so I wandered around her room, touching things. Her walls were covered with posters of Riley Rivers. Even her bedspread had a life-sized picture of Riley printed on it. I ran my hand across the clothes in her closet. Everything smelled like the strawberry-flavoured lip balm she wore. Jim didn't let her wear makeup, so she went crazy for the strawberry lip balm. Her desk was pristine, as if it never got used. The only thing on it was the Riley Rivers magazine I gave her. I flipped through the pages and pressed the photos to my cheek. Nothing worked, so I flopped down on her bed, hugged a pink, heart-shaped pillow and stared at the ceiling.

Why didn't I try harder to find out the guy's real identity when I first had suspicions? Why didn't I go after her to calm her down when she was angry at me? Why did I go to Squamish and leave him unsupervised around her? I couldn't even comfort myself by saying I didn't know something bad was going to happen, because I did. What was the point of seeing her face? It wasn't to prevent it or it would have been more specific. There had to be another explanation.

Frustrated with myself for not being able to control my stupid brain glitch, I got up and left her room. The most useful thing I could think to do was bake apple cinnamon muffins and fill the coffee urn for the volunteers, which wasn't at all useful, but better than nothing. I headed back to the Inn and got to work. As I was removing the muffin trays from the oven, someone entered the kitchen behind me, so I turned. Mom was standing with her arms open for a hug. I ran over and let her squeeze me tightly. "I'm sorry I yelled at you on the phone."

"It's okay, honey. You've got a lot going on. Grandpa called to tell me about Kailyn." She kissed the top of my head, then released me from the hug. "Jim and Trevor must be going out of their minds with worry. What can I do to help?"

"I don't think there is much anybody can do until the police track the driver down. I was just putting some snacks together for the volunteers as a way to keep myself busy. If you want to help, you can fill those baskets with apples, bananas, and oranges. I'll take the water and juice out onto the deck."

She smiled sympathetically and got to work.

"Thanks for coming up. Did you drive?"

"I got a ride."

I was going to ask who drove her, but I knew it was the new boyfriend and I really wasn't in the right mood to meet him. Instead of asking for details I nodded and picked up the flats to carry them outside. Trevor crossed the parking lot and approached me with a hopeful expression.

"It wasn't working," I said. "Sorry."

"It's okay."

It wasn't okay. I knew that. Long shot or not, a vision was the best chance we had of finding her before it was too late. It killed me to let him down. "I'm hoping it will hit me randomly if I stay busy."

"Do whatever feels right. And if nothing comes, don't worry about it. What's supposed to happen will happen."

I wasn't okay with that. If what was supposed to happen was Kailyn getting hurt, I would do everything in my power to prevent that. "Maybe I should go into the forest where it's quiet."

"Take a look at this first." Trevor stepped onto the deck and sat against the railing. "A guy who fits the description you gave was pulling a dice-sliding scam at the casino and they have him on video. They've released a police bulletin."

"Do they know if she's with him?"

He shook his head. "Not yet. Maybe if you look at the photo of him it will trigger something."

I stepped in to lean against his chest as he showed me the police bulletin on his phone. He wrapped his arm around me and held me tight as I stared at the guy's beady eyes. I wished with all my heart that I could see something and take away the pain Trevor was feeling. If Kailyn wasn't found safe, the only thing I would be able to do is be patient and unwavering as he picked up the pieces of his life—the same way he had done for me. I wished he would never feel something that tragic, but I didn't see anything. His phone screen faded to black.

I sighed. "Sorry."

His head dropped and he kissed my forehead tenderly. Then his attention shifted to someone who stepped out onto the deck. I turned. My mom took a second to absorb the sight of us embracing, then she asked with a slight tone of disapproval, "You two are a couple now?"

Neither one of us answered because we hadn't actually established that, but he hugged me tight to his side.

"You're still going to Toronto, though. Right?" she asked me, but it sounded more like a demand.

I glanced at Trevor because we hadn't covered that in the discussion process yet either. "I want to stay here. Everyone I know is here."

"Seriously? So, you're going to throw away a ten-thousand-dollar scholarship for a rock-star-wannabee girlfriend who doesn't even plan to go to university and an adrenaline-junkie boyfriend who will live in Britannia Beach for the rest of his life?" She threw her hands up in the air in exaggerated surrender. "I'm not going to tell you what to do. But you might want to be really sure about that decision before you close doors to opportunities."

"Mom. Kailyn is missing. The school I choose is so unimportant right now."

She shook her head, still angry, but accepting that it was not the best time to discuss it, and then disappeared back into the kitchen.

I rolled my eyes and crossed my arms. "God. She has a talent for pissing me off."

"You never told me the scholarship is worth ten thousand dollars," Trevor said.

"Does it matter?"

He turned and leaned against the porch with his arms braced tensely. "It's a lot of money to turn down."

I frowned and studied his expression. I didn't like what I saw. He was having second thoughts, and it was my mom's fault. "The amount of the scholarship isn't important right now. Can we talk about it after we find Kailyn? Making sure she's safe is all we should be focused on."

He nodded to agree, then stepped down off the deck and crossed the lot to stand with Murphy next to a police cruiser. After some debate, Jim made the decision to have the team go to the gas station in Whistler where the car had been abandoned and launch a search from there. Trevor walked over to leave a police scanner with me. "Do you mind staying here in case she comes home on her own?"

"Of course. Be safe. I'll keep trying to see something." I leaned over the railing to give him a quick kiss, then he got in his truck and followed the rest of the team out onto the highway.

After the village was back to its quiet norm, it felt eerie. And the chatter on the scanner echoed against the mountain. Mom stepped out onto the porch and rested her palms on the railing, staring up at the trees. "I overreacted earlier about you dating Trevor. I'm sorry."

"It's okay. We're all under a lot of stress." Even though I meant what I said and I was glad she was with me, the resentment I felt towards her was still so strong. It wasn't healthy. And it really wasn't serving any purpose besides deteriorating our relationship. I wanted to let it go and repair things between us. "I want to apologize to you."

She turned to face me and leaned her hips against the railing. "You don't need to apologize. If you want to go to UBC and date Trevor I support you one hundred percent. I was just surprised at first. But then, once I thought about it some more, it made perfect sense. I would be happy if you stayed, especially if that's what would make you happy. I also understand why you aren't comfortable with the idea of me dating again. I wasn't even sure if I was ready for it yet. Don't worry about that right now. There is no need to rush into any of that with all the other changes that have been going on."

"Actually, I'm sorry for something else. Something you don't know about. Something from the past I haven't been able to forgive you for."

She hugged herself as if she felt a breeze, but maybe she was bracing in anticipation of an emotional body blow. "Are you angry because I haven't visited you here more often?"

I shook my head and leaned forward to rest my elbows on my knees. "No. I was already used to you not being here that often."

"I'm sorry I left you here alone with the responsibility of keeping Grandpa company and helping out at the Inn."

"It's not that. I liked doing those things."

She studied my expression, then glanced over the parking lot towards the water. "Is it something I can fix or make amends for?"

"No."

Her head shifted back and she made eye contact with me. "Then where does that leave us now?"

"I don't know." I stood and walked over to lean against the

railing next to her. "All I know is that I need to figure out how to forgive you for something that wasn't your fault. And then I need to let it go so we can move forward. It's my issue to work out, not yours. I just wanted to let you know that I am determined to make things better."

She wrapped her arms around me and pulled me in tight to rest her cheek on top of my head. "You blame me for what happened to your dad, don't you?"

I clenched my eyes shut.

She was quiet for a couple of breaths, then, to my surprise, she whispered, "I understand if you do. I do, too, sweetie. I do, too."

Hearing her say it out loud and knowing that she struggled with the guilt instantly flooded me with sympathy and remorse. It really wasn't her fault. He just happened to be going to Vancouver to see her on the day the accident happened. The truth was there were a lot of people to blame—myself for not recognizing his face in the vision in time to warn him, the semi-truck driver who jack-knifed, or the road engineers who didn't make the guardrail stronger. But she had been the person I blamed the most because she insisted on living in the city. It could have happened on his way to work or to go grocery shopping, though.

As I rested in her embrace the anger dissipated, but then sadness took its place, which was definitely the more painful of the two emotions. Eventually I said, "I don't want to blame anyone anymore."

"Me neither. Let's start fresh."

I nodded and she started to cry, so she kissed my cheek and then excused herself and went inside. It felt good to forgive her, but that meant I was the only one left to forgive. That was going to be much harder.

Kailyn's Kiki keychain was still in my pocket, so I took it out and squeezed it in my palm. When we were younger, Kailyn really wanted to do all the things Trevor and I did. Sometimes she wasn't allowed because it wasn't safe, but usually it was because Jim was overly cautious and hesitant to let her try. When she turned sixteen he gave her her own keys to the house, which she felt symbolized adult responsibilities and some of the freedom she had been wishing for. She was so excited, so Trevor carved her the custom keychain for her birthday. She lost her keys fairly regularly, but because of the keychain they always got returned. As I traced my finger over each letter, I had a vision: Kailyn stepped down narrow steps and through a glass door. Then the scene changed. It was dark and really loud. People crowded around us. She pressed her hands over her ears to block the noise before she turned and grinned at me.

The vision ended and I fumbled to text Trevor: *I saw her get off a bus. Not sure where or when. Then she was somewhere dark and crowded.*

*Ok. Good job. I'll let the cops know.*

I closed my eyes to concentrate. I recognized the glass door Kailyn walked through. I had done it so many times myself when I went to visit my mom. It looked like the Whistler-Squamish-Vancouver bus I always took. Kailyn could have been headed north to Whistler or south to Vancouver. The team was already searching north so I decided to head south. It was possible if I was physically in Vancouver the surroundings would trigger another vision with more details. It was worth a try. I stood and dialled the number of the only person who could get me there fast enough to check it out. Mason answered.

"I am so sorry to bother you at work, but it's an emergency," I said.

"What's wrong?"

"Trevor's sister went missing and I just had a vision of her on a bus. She might have been headed to Vancouver and I think I need to be there to see more. I know it sounds crazy. But is there any way you can send your dad's helicopter to Britannia Beach to pick me up? I need to get downtown as fast as possible."

Without even asking for more details, he said, "Yeah, it's already at the house because my dad has to be at the airport. It can be there in three minutes to pick you up."

"Perfect. Thank you. I owe you."

I grabbed a jacket and my purse and ran towards the highway. Once there was a break in the traffic I ran across the lanes. I jumped over the railroad tracks and scrambled down the rocks onto the sand. The helicopter landed on the dock as I hurried, bent over, towards it.

Mason's dad was waiting inside. "Where to?" he asked.

# CHAPTER 23

We couldn't land exactly where I wanted to go, so the pilot communicated on the radio to find a helicopter pad nearby. We were able to land on a rooftop just down the street. I thanked Mr. Cartwright and hopped off the helicopter, then it took off again to head to the airport.

I rushed across the roof, took the elevator down to the ground floor, and then ran along the sidewalk to the bus stop I used when I visited my mom. It was the only one I had ever taken Kailyn to. She wasn't anywhere on the sidewalk, so I hurried down the stairs into the SkyTrain station and wove through the crowds of people flowing the other way. I bought a ticket so I could search the train platforms, but she wasn't there. She wasn't in the bathrooms either.

Mason texted me: *Are you at Waterfront?*

*No. The Squamish bus stops at Burrard Station. She's not here.*

He responded immediately: *I'll hop in a cab and meet you there to help search.*

*Thanks.* I appreciated his offer. Unfortunately, it probably wouldn't help that much to have two people looking if we didn't know where she went. I headed back up the stairs onto street level and wandered around, poking my head in cafés as I waited for Mason.

If she did come down on the bus she could have gone anywhere. Especially if the guy was with her. He could have taken her on a train, in a cab, or had someone else pick them up. The possibilities were endless. And terrifying.

A yellow cab pulled up to the curb and Mason hopped out. He hugged me and then waited for me to tell him what I wanted to do next. I didn't know. I sat on a bench and watched the people file out of the train station. Seeing her get off the bus wasn't a specific enough clue.

Mason sat next to me. "Can you think of any reason why she would come to Vancouver—maybe a friend she would visit or a place she likes to go to?"

An analytical approach. Yes, that was good. Places she might want to go if she made the trip under her own power. "Um, she used to love the aquarium, but she sort of outgrew that. Sometimes she likes it when I take her shopping on Robson Street. Other than that she doesn't really like being in the city. It's too loud and crowded for her."

"Do you want to walk up to Robson?"

I sighed and heaved myself off the bench. It felt like we'd have as much luck running into her on Robson as finding a specific grain of sand on the beach, but we had to try. And maybe I would see something as we walked the five blocks over to the shopping district. We split up and made our way along the strip of stores on both sides of the street, asking sales clerks if they'd seen her. I showed her picture to a motorcycle cop who was writing out a parking ticket. He said he'd contact me if he saw her.

Discouraged by the enormity of possibilities, I sat on a concrete planter to think.

Mason bought a coffee at the shop on the corner and brought me a tea. He sat next to me and smiled in an encouraging way.

"Sorry to waste your time. I know you have a lot of work to do. You can go back to your office. I'll keep looking by myself for a while and then take transit back home."

"This is more important than work." He wrapped his arm around my shoulders. "It's not a waste of time. We just need a little more to go on."

I nodded, feeling pressured by the minutes ticking by. There was a possibility she was getting farther and farther away by the second. And her time was running out if the guy planned to hurt her. "I need to see the next clue."

He was quiet to let me concentrate. When nothing happened I groaned with frustration and paced around.

"How did you see the bus clue?"

"I was holding her keychain." I held it up to show him I was already trying that one again, with no success. "I wish I had more control over it."

"According to some of the literature it can be practiced and honed like any other talent."

"You researched it?"

"Yeah, after our picnic I went home and studied up on intuition and psychic ability. It's extremely interesting. According to some of the articles it's not really scientifically accepted, but I found a lot of valid evidence written about clairvoyants, empaths, and lucid dreaming. And police forces use psychics to help in investigations, so there's obviously something to it."

"Thanks for being open-minded. Most people don't believe it's possible."

"Well, I've seen you do it, which is all the evidence I need. Just be patient. Something will come to you."

"I hope so." I sat back down and took a sip of tea. "I don't think I can live with the guilt of not being able to save another person I love in time."

"Actually, I've been thinking a lot about your dad's accident since our picnic, too."

It was touching that he cared, but I wasn't in the right mood to talk about my dad, so I took another sip of tea and watched the traffic go by.

"Maybe you didn't see your dad's accident beforehand so you could prevent it."

"Trevor has said that a thousand times, trying to help me forgive myself. He has always said that some things in life are meant to happen no matter what we do."

"Well, he's right. Everything happens for a reason."

"That might be true, but it doesn't make me feel any better. What is the reason for me seeing something ahead of time if there is nothing that can be done about it?"

"You know how you said I was meant to be with Cody when he passed away so he wouldn't be afraid? Maybe you saw the accident so you would have a way to be there with your dad in his last moments. So the last thing he felt was your love."

Bursts of electricity erupted across the surface of my skin and gave me goose bumps as his words sunk in. I had never thought of it that way before, but it made sense. He was right. It wasn't until after the police notified us of what happened that I actually saw my dad's face in the vision. Prior to that I had only seen the view from the windshield. Emotion flooded into my chest and inched up into my throat as I closed my eyes and replayed the images of the accident. It was as if I was in the passenger seat. The semi jack-knifed and my dad swerved. The car broke through the guardrail. And as we flew through the air, my dad reached over and held my hand. He smiled at me one last time. Then I was ripped from the car and viewing the accident from the highway, looking down into the ravine. The car crumpled against a tree, then tumbled down the cliff onto the rocks below.

Mason's eyes filled with empathy as he watched my reaction.

Oh my God. I had tried a million times to come to terms with the guilt. If that was the reason I didn't see my dad's face beforehand that changed everything. It brought me so much peace to know I saw it so I could be close to him and be able to say good-bye one last time. "Thank you, Mason."

He reached over and brushed my cheek with the back of his hand. "You're welcome."

My relief was replaced with panic when I realized that maybe the reason I had seen Kailyn's smiling face was so I could be there with her in her last moments of life, too. I stood and paced, pulling at chunks of my hair. "We have to find her."

My phone buzzed with a message from Trevor: *They arrested the guy in Pemberton. Kailyn wasn't with him. Have you seen anything else that might help?*

Before I had a chance to reply, a car drove by with the windows down and the radio playing. It was a song I'd heard Doug sing before. Not one of the band's songs. One of Riley Rivers' songs. I saw her smiling face again. It was dark, loud, and crowded. And that song was playing. "Oh my God, I think I know why she wanted to come to Vancouver." I checked my theory on my phone and then texted Trevor back: *I'm going to check something. I'll keep you updated.* I pulled Mason by the hand and hailed a cab from the curb. "I think she might have been headed to the stadium, if she made it safely."

The cab ride was quick and the driver parked in a loading zone on the lower level of the stadium. Mason paid the fare and I ran towards the entrance gates. The concourse was completely packed with screaming teenage girls. Mason caught up to me. Thankfully, he was taller than all the kids and he scanned the crowd looking for Kailyn. The swarm of girls were already in a frenzy. When Mason walked between them they kind of lost it because he was hot enough to be a teen idol.

Searching the face of every blonde girl was time-consuming and felt futile since they were all moving around and the crowd was continually getting larger as more fans arrived. It took a long time, but Mason finally spotted Kailyn sitting on the ground with her back rested against the wall. She was looking at a picture of Riley Rivers and eating a granola bar.

I wiped the tears of relief that had pooled along my lashes and rushed over to her. "Kailyn."

"Derian! You came to see Riley Rivers, too."

"Actually, I came to find you." I sat down on the ground beside her and stretched my arm across her shoulders. "Your dad and Trevor think you're lost because you forgot to tell them you were coming here. We were worried you went with the man at the hotel."

"The bad man wanted to drive me."

"He dropped you off here?"

"No. I said he can't drive me unless my dad says it's okay."

"What happened after you told him no? Did he hurt you at all?"

"No. He drove away fast before I could ask my dad. I took the bus instead."

I squeezed her tightly, so thankful she was okay. "That was smart to say you needed to check with your dad first. I'm really glad you didn't get a ride with him, but you didn't need to take the bus all alone. You could have asked me. I would have brought you to the concert."

She frowned when she noticed Mason standing ten metres away. "I'm a grown-up. I can go on the bus by myself."

"I know. Just maybe tell someone next time."

"Fine," she said as she clutched her ticket to the concert.

"Why aren't you answering your phone?"

"The battery died."

I pulled out my phone. It only rang once before Trevor picked up. "I found her in Vancouver waiting for the Riley Rivers concert. The guy had offered to give her a ride but took off when she told him she would have to ask your dad first. She rode the bus down by herself. I'm with her. She's safe."

He exhaled and paused in silence for a second before he choked out, "You're the best, Deri. Thank you." Then I heard him pass the phone off.

The voice that came on was Murphy's. "Hello?"

"Hi, Murph. It's Derian. Is Trevor okay?"

"I don't know. He just gave me the phone and disappeared. What did you say to him?"

"I found Kailyn. I had a vision she was at the stadium for a concert. She's with me. She's safe."

"All right. Good job, Deri. Hold on." He shouted away from the phone, "Derian found her." Then he spoke back to me, "Jim wants to talk to Kailyn." I handed the phone to Kailyn and listened to her half of the conversation.

"Hi Daddy. Are you mad at me? … No! I'm a grown-up… No… Okay… No… I'm sorry… No, Derian is going to come with me to the Riley Rivers concert." She looked over at me to make sure that was right. I nodded and she went back to talking to her dad. "Okay… I know… don't be sad. I'm not hurt… I didn't mean to scare you… Oh, okay. I know, Derian told me I have to tell someone where I'm going… Okay. I love you and I love Trevor. I'm going to marry Riley Rivers." She handed the phone back to me and said, "Daddy wants to talk to you."

"Hello," I said.

"You did good, kid." He sounded as choked up as Trevor and struggled to keep it together long enough to say, "Thank you."

I started to say, "You're welcome," but he had passed the phone away before I even got it out.

"Me again," Murphy joked. "These Maverty men can't keep their shit together. We'll be here when you get back. Your Spidey senses are pretty impressive. Maybe a hero's welcome is in order."

"No. Don't," I warned.

"Easy, I'm joking. By the way, you might want to leave helicopter boy back in Vancouver if you don't want Trevor to snap."

"I wouldn't have found her without his help."

"Exactly. He helped you do what we all wish we could have done. Think about it."

I hung up and Mason approached us, putting his phone away.

He smiled at me and tilted his head towards the private suites entrance. "We have a corporate box if you want to have dinner before the show." He winked. "And I made some special arrangements for afterwards."

"Come on, Kiki, Mason has a very big surprise for you." I helped her get up and arrange all her things back into her backpack. We took a private elevator to the box suites and when we got to the door the usher said, "Welcome Mr. Cartwright, Ms. Lafleur, and Ms. Maverty. Order whatever you would like off the menu. Then enjoy the show."

Kailyn pressed her fists into her cheeks and squealed.

# CHAPTER 24

The concert was actually pretty fun. Kailyn was having the time of her life. I had to grab the back of her belt a couple of times because I was worried she was going to lean too far forward over the railing and fall. Mason sat beside me, smiling.

He had arranged for Kailyn to go backstage and meet Riley after the concert. She went absolutely berserk when she got her picture taken with him. He was a nice guy and he signed all her stuff. He also drew a heart on her t-shirt with their initials in it. I thought I was going to have to pick her off the ceiling. Security eventually rushed Riley off, so Kailyn and I went back to where Mason was waiting in the airlock.

Kailyn hugged him. "Thank you Mason Cartwright. This was the best day of my life. I love you."

"You're welcome." He hugged her back and smiled in the most genuine way.

The fact that he was so generous and sweet was actually heartbreaking. It made what needed to come next painful to even think about. I dreaded every step of the three-block walk back to his office. It had to be done. Be honest. Be fair to him. Be mature. Ugh. I wished I didn't have to.

The helicopter was already on the roof and the pilot was

waiting for us. Kailyn climbed in, covered her ears, and screeched as she rocked back and forth in her seat. I paused and turned to face Mason, wringing my hands nervously. Do it now, Deri. Privately. Before we get back to Britannia Beach. "Thank you for the concert and dinner. It meant so much to her to meet him. You are seriously the most generous person I know. And thank you for helping me find her. I can't even tell you how grateful I am for that."

"I'm happy I could help. Anytime you need anything just ask." He leaned in as if he planned to kiss me and I pulled back to dodge it. The smile dropped off his face, then recognition flickered in his eyes when he figured it out. He ran his hand through his hair and looked out at the city skyline. "There is something going on between you and Trevor, isn't there?"

I exhaled slowly. "Yes. I'm sorry."

He nodded as if he accepted the truth but wasn't particularly happy about it. "Well, I'm disappointed, obviously. But I'm not surprised. Thanks for being honest." He stepped back. "You guys head home without me. I need to get some work done."

Struck by the change in his tone, I scrambled to make things right and dislodge the guilt that embedded into my heart like barbed wire. "I know this sounds lame but I would really like to still be friends. If it's okay with you. What you said about my dad is going to change my life. It already has. I feel lucky to know you."

He nodded, but didn't actually say he wanted to stay friends.

The silence got awkward, so I reached around to find the latch of the necklace he gave me. "I should give this back to you."

"Don't. It was a gift. I want you to have it."

I frowned because it felt final. Like he didn't want a friendship. Like we would never see each other again. That wasn't what I wanted, but it wasn't really my choice. "I won't ever forget you. Thank you. For everything."

"You're welcome. Take care." He hugged me once more before he turned and walked away. That fast. Like everything between us meant nothing. It was just over. I knew it wasn't fair to ask him to still be friends when he wanted, and deserved, more. But the selfish side of me wished I could keep him in my life. I watched him disappear through the building door. He didn't look back and I felt an instant loss. I sighed and climbed back on board.

Kailyn rocked and clenched her eyes shut the entire flight home. When we landed on the dock in Britannia Beach, three flashlights bounced across the highway. It was Murphy, Trevor, and his dad. I thanked the pilot and helped Kailyn get out. Jim almost threw himself at Kailyn and swung her around like a little kid. Trevor kissed her forehead and then walked towards me as Murphy rushed forward and gave Kailyn one of his bear hugs. Trevor glanced briefly into the helicopter, obviously to check if Mason was with us. Then he turned to me, leaned in close to my ear and said, "Thanks for finding her."

I nodded as the helicopter took off and almost blew us over. Jim and Murphy helped Kailyn climb down off the dock and cross the sand towards the railroad tracks. Trevor's hands slid up to cradle my face. I couldn't see his expression, but I could tell by his silence and the tension in his muscles that he was feeling overwhelmed.

Standing there in the dark, surrounded by everything that was familiar and comfortable—Britannia Beach, the Inn, the mountains, the ocean, the dock, and Trevor— I knew that my entire life was about to change. There was a whole other world out there. And no matter what the future held, the one thing that was certain was my time in Britannia Beach was coming to an end.

I closed my eyes to listen to the water lapping against the rocks. My lungs filled with the fresh forest air. And then I ran my palm across Trevor's chest and rested it over his heart. The beat was strong and steady. Unwavering.

With my eyes still shut, I whispered, "Now what?"

The End of Book Two

# ACKNOWLEDGEMENTS

None of my books would be possible without the support of my husband Sean and the rest of my family. Thank you to my critique partner Denise Jaden, Greg Ng (and the moms from his class who volunteered to read a very early rough draft of this story), Rasadi Cortes, Erica Ediger, Jen Wilson, Belinda Wagner, Lisa Marks, Cory Cavazzi, my mom and dad, my brother Rob, my sister Luan, my editors Charlotte Ledger and Laura McCallen, and the entire team behind the scenes at Harper*Impulse* and HarperCollins*Publishers*. I'd also like to send a special thank-you to the real Search and Rescue volunteers and first responders in the Squamish area, and the young adult bloggers and youth librarians who tirelessly introduce books to young readers.